The revelations about her father, mother and grandmother haunted her. How could she have never known the truth? Why hadn't anyone told her until now?

"You should have been the one to tell me," Leah said to her mother, knowing she sounded hurt. "Why am I always the last to know about everything in this family?"

"It isn't a conspiracy, Leah. I was going to tell you about your father. I just never knew how."

UNTIL
ANGELS
CLOSE MY
EYES

Lurlene McDaniel

UNTIL ANGELS CLOSE MY EYES

BANTAM BOOKS

NEW YORK • TORONTO • LONDON • SYDNEY • AUCKLAND

RL 4.7, AGES 012 AND UP

UNTIL ANGELS CLOSE MY EYES

A Bantam Book / August 1998

The Starfire logo is a registered trademark of Bantam Books, a division of Bantam Doubleday Dell Publishing Group, Inc. Registered in U.S. Patent and Trademark Office and elsewhere.

Scripture quotations marked (NIV) are from the Holy Bible, New International Version. Copyright © 1973, 1978, 1984 by International Bible Society. Used by permission of Zondervan Bible Publishers.

All rights reserved.
Text copyright © 1998 by Lurlene McDaniel.
Cover art copyright © 1998 by Kamil Vojnar.
All rights reserved. No part of this book may be reproduced or transmitted in any form or by any means, electronic or mechanical, including photocopying, recording, or by any information storage and retrieval system, without permission in writing from the publisher. For information address: Bantam Doubleday Dell Books for Young Readers.

If you purchased this book without a cover you should be aware that this book is stolen property. It was reported as "unsold and destroyed" to the publisher and neither the author nor the publisher has received any payment for this "stripped book."

ISBN 0-553-57115-X

Published simultaneously in the United States and Canada

Bantam Books are published by Bantam Books, a division of Bantam Doubleday Dell Publishing Group, Inc. Its trademark, consisting of the words "Bantam Books" and the portrayal of a rooster, is Registered in U.S. Patent and Trademark Office and in other countries. Marca Registrada. Bantam Books, 1540 Broadway, New York, New York 10036.

PRINTED IN THE UNITED STATES OF AMERICA

OPM   20   19   18   17   16   15   14   13   12

This book is dedicated to
Josiah Christian McDaniel,
a lamb of God.

"What is man that you are mindful of him,
the son of man that you care for him?
You made him a little lower than the
    angels;
you crowned him with glory and honor
and put everything under his feet."

(HEBREWS 2: 6–8, NIV)

ONE

"Leah, we need to talk."

Leah Lewis-Hall flicked off the TV and gave her mother her full attention. "What's up?" She knew something was wrong. For days, her mother had seemed edgy and uncommunicative. Most unlike herself. Leah's mother usually had something to say about everything. When Leah had come home from school that day, the house had been empty and there had only been a terse note: *Neil and I will be back before supper.*

Her mother sat down on the edge of the sofa. "I'm sure you've noticed that things haven't been exactly normal around here lately."

"Are you and Neil having problems?" Leah asked, fearing the worst. Since Neil was husband number five for her mother, Leah had reason to feel apprehensive. *Don't let it be divorce,* she pleaded silently. She liked Neil. A lot. He was the best stepfather she had ever had. Not only that, but she didn't want to be uprooted and moved again. Not in her senior year. It was only October. Couldn't her mother at least gut it out until June?

"Yes, we're having problems," her mother said.

"What's wrong?" Leah's heart sank.

Her mother stood, wrung her hands, and began pacing the living room floor. "Neil had a doctor's appointment last week. Then, today, we went back for a consultation."

"Where is Neil anyway?" All at once Leah realized that Neil was not in the house.

"He's been checked into the hospital."

"What?" Leah's heart began to thud. "Is he sick? What's happened?" She knew a lot

about being sick. Almost a year before, Leah had been diagnosed with bone cancer. Leah's mother had all but threatened the doctor with a lawsuit for incompetence and a misdiagnosis. Now her mother looked ghastly pale. Her face reminded Leah of her own excruciating experience.

"I—I never told you something about Neil when he and I first got married," her mother said, her voice quivering. "When Neil and I first met back in Dallas, when we first started dating, I never dreamed it would lead to marriage. He knew I didn't have a great track record when it came to matrimony. But we fell in love. I want you to remember that. I love Neil very much. Even the age difference between us never mattered to me."

Leah thought she might scream, waiting for her mother to get to the point.

"When things first started getting serious between us, Neil confided that he had a serious medical problem. It began even before his first wife died. Leah, Neil was diagnosed with cancer in one of his kidneys."

"*Cancer?* Neil has cancer? What are you telling me?" Leah's voice was trembling.

"Calm down, Leah, please. The affected kidney was removed and he went through chemotherapy to destroy any lingering malignant cells. He's never had another problem. I just assumed he was cured. You know how doctors are."

Leah was reeling, unable to absorb all the emotions that were shooting through her. "You're telling me that Neil Dutton, my stepfather, has had cancer? Why didn't you ever *tell* me? I should have been told, Mother. Especially with my condition."

"We were going to tell you. But the timing was just never right. We were going to tell you when we got back from our honeymoon in Japan. But then you were in the hospital, and Dr. Thomas insisted that you had cancer. We thought it best not to tell you then."

Leah's stay in the hospital had been traumatic. First the diagnosis of cancer. Then the appearance, to Leah anyway, of the mysterious Gabriella, followed by the strange and seemingly impossible retreat of the cancer from Leah's leg bone. She had undergone six long weeks of chemotherapy and still returned to her doctor for periodic workups and evaluations. "I can't believe this! You had plenty of opportunities to say something about this."

"Neil didn't want to. He thought it best for you to concentrate on getting through chemo. And when that was over, he didn't want to burden you."

By now Leah was on her feet. "Burden me? How can you say such a thing? Even if Neil didn't tell me, you should have, Mom. It was *your* place to tell me!" She stopped abruptly. A new fear gripped her, overshadowing her anger. She turned to face her mother. "So why is Neil in the hospital?"

Her mother's chin began to tremble. "Because it appears his cancer has recurred."

Leah moved around her bedroom as if in a trance, preparing to go with her mother to the hospital to see Neil. She could hear her mother crying in the bathroom down the hall. *This can't be happening,* she kept telling herself.

She stopped at the window and stared out at the twilight. The farm fields stretched into the distance, broken only by a line of trees whose leaves were shot through with red and gold. It seemed all the leaves were on the brink of death.

Leah longed to talk to Ethan. He would help her sort everything out. The clear image of his tanned face, eyes as blue as sky, hair the color of wheat and sunlight, seemed to smile back at her from the window.

"I love you, Leah," he had told her that last afternoon they'd been together in August. But he was Amish, she was English. They were worlds apart in every way— miles apart physically. Yet she ached to see him, touch him. She missed him. She missed the rest of his family, too, especially his sisters Charity and Rebekah. Leah shook her head sadly. She'd never see Rebekah again—at least, not in this world.

Leah leaned her forehead against the cool pane. She had no way of getting hold of Ethan. The Amish had no phones, no computers for E-mail, no fax machines. Only snail mail, the U.S. postal system. Although she'd write him that very night to tell him about Neil, it would take days for him to get her letter and respond. She needed him now. No one at her new school would understand what she was going through. She wasn't particularly close to anybody there. Sure, she had friends, but no one as special as Ethan.

"Are you ready?"

Her mother's question brought Leah back to the moment. "Sure. Let's go."

They didn't talk during the fifteen-minute ride to the hospital. Leah knew what it was like to hear doctors say, "You have cancer." And apparently, so did Neil. At the moment, Leah just wanted to see him with her own eyes.

The community hospital wasn't huge, but it was new. As she stepped into the hospital corridor, Leah's own hospital stay in Indianapolis flooded back to her. The smell was the same: clean and antiseptic.

Leah's mother stepped up to the nurse's station. "I'm Roberta Dutton. Has the doctor been in to see my husband yet?" she asked.

"Dr. Howser is in with Mr. Dutton now," the nurse said.

Leah remembered Dr. Howser, Neil's physician. She had gone to see him when her finger broke for no apparent reason while Neil and her mother were honeymooning in Japan. Dr. Howser had X-rayed the finger, then sent her off to the hospital in Indianapolis. Except for meeting the Amish family she never would otherwise have known, the experience had been horrifying.

Leah's mother stopped in front of a door, squared her shoulders and pasted a smile on her face. She breezed into the room, and Leah followed.

Neil was propped up in the hospital bed. "Hey, girls," he said as Roberta kissed him on the cheek. Neil was sixty-eight, but he had always looked and acted much younger. The beautiful tan he'd gotten aboard the windjammer the past summer was gone. His skin looked sallow and papery. Leah swallowed against a lump in her throat. This change hadn't happened overnight, and she was upset with herself for not noticing it before.

"Look, why don't I let you visit with your family, Neil," Dr. Howser said. "I'll see you tomorrow when I make my rounds."

"As soon as I'm out of here, let's hit a few golf balls." Neil's voice had a forced joviality to it.

"You got it," Dr. Howser said before slipping out.

Leah's mother settled on the bed and took Neil's hand. "How are you feeling, dear?"

"Like a truck ran over me."

Leah noticed big bruises on Neil's arms.

Neil pushed his reading glasses down his nose and looked over them at Leah. "Hi, Leah. How are you?" His voice sounded kind, soft.

Leah felt glued to the floor.

"Come closer, honey."

Stiffly she edged forward. "I'm sorry you're sick," she mumbled.

Neil studied her, then turned to his wife. "Roberta, why don't you go get Leah and me some ice cream in the cafeteria? I couldn't eat much supper, and ice cream would taste good to me now."

The request almost made Leah start crying. She and Neil sometimes ate ice cream and watched TV together in the evenings at home.

Roberta glanced between Neil and Leah. "I guess I could." She stood hesitantly, looking a little lost. Leah kept staring at Neil. Her tears had retreated. In their place was a building bubble of anger.

When Roberta finally left the room, Neil held out his hand. "Come closer, Leah."

She shook her head furiously.

"Please."

Tears formed again in Leah's eyes. She threw her coat on the floor and hurled herself at his bedside. "Why!" she exploded. "Why didn't you tell me you had cancer? Why didn't you tell me the truth?"

TWO

Neil calmly patted the mattress. "Come sit down, Leah. I sent your mother out of the room so that we could talk."

"I don't want to sit down." Leah was shaking. She hugged her arms to herself.

"I want to explain why I kept this from you, but I can't talk to you when you're hating me for it."

"I don't hate you. Please tell me."

"In a nutshell, the timing never seemed right. And don't be mad at your mother—I swore her to secrecy."

It irritated Leah that Neil knew just what she was thinking. She *was* angry at her mother. "I'm angry at you, too," she said.

"I knew you would be." He gave her an apologetic smile. "But please put yourself in my place for a minute. When you were first told about your cancer, you and I were virtual strangers. I'd just married your mother, you weren't happy about being moved from Dallas to Indiana farm country, and I was adjusting to taking on a wife and an almost grown daughter."

Neil's assessment was correct. Leah had hated moving and starting over in another school—especially one out in the boondocks.

Neil continued. "My first wife and I never had children, but I'd always wanted them. Suddenly, in my twilight years, I had a young energetic wife and a lovely stepdaughter. I was a little overwhelmed. I didn't want us to start out as enemies, Leah. I knew I wasn't your biological father, and I knew I couldn't replace him. I had to find my own place with you."

Leah turned her head, not wanting Neil to see how quickly tears had sprung to her eyes at the mention of her father. He'd died years before, homeless and on the streets. Her only link with him had been her Grandma Hall, but she had died too, and the biological link had been forever severed. Leah's mother had married and divorced three more times before marrying Neil. "What do you want me to say?" Leah asked, looking right at Neil. "That I like you better than the others?"

He smiled wryly. "Just that you like me is good enough."

"You know I like you. So if you know it, you should have said something about your cancer to me. You knew what I was going through."

"It was a judgment call. At the time, the last thing I thought you needed to hear was a lame pep talk, like, 'Oh, by the way, I've had cancer myself, so hang tough and make it through just like I did.' I thought you needed to hear that I cared about you regardless of any health problems, and that your mother and I were going to be around for you no matter what. I see now that it was a poor call. I'm sorry."

"Well, when I started chemo, you should have told me then. I was scared. You could have helped me."

"I almost did," Neil said with a sigh. "But I was afraid of discouraging you. You see, I was so sick during my chemo treatments six years ago that I wanted to die. When I saw you going through chemo, I figured, why tell you about my horrors when you were having hardly any problems with it. I didn't want to jinx you."

Except for some mild nausea, Leah had sailed through chemo treatments. "So that's why you didn't say anything? You didn't want to give off negative vibes?" she said, rolling her eyes.

"You did have a pretty easy time with it, Leah. You never even lost your hair. I was bald as a cue ball for months."

Leah tried to picture Neil without his head of steely white hair. "All right," she said grudgingly. "What about after my chemo? You could have told me then."

"Again, I could have, but I didn't. I gave you the car to celebrate." He smiled again. "I wanted you to be happy, and telling you then seemed impossible. I wanted to have more in common with you than cancer."

Leah felt exasperated by his explanations. His logic did sound . . . well, logical. However, she was still angry and didn't want to let him off the hook for keeping such a secret from her. "You still should have said something to me."

"I really figured I'd tell you this past summer. Out there on that windjammer, under those stars, a person feels very close to God. And to one's family."

"I wanted to live in Nappanee and work," Leah said defensively. She didn't add that she'd wanted to be with Ethan as much as possible, and that her summer with him had been wonderful.

"And I agreed that you should," Neil said. "Didn't I argue in your favor?"

It was true. It had been Neil who'd gone to bat for Leah with her mother. It had been Neil who'd found her a job and a place to live. "I came home in August," she said, getting in one more dig.

"And you were heartbroken over the

death of little Rebekah. How could I have added to your pain?" Neil asked. "I couldn't."

"But now you're sick and I *have* to know. Otherwise, you'd probably never have told me, would you?"

"Probably not," Neil said. "By now, it would have been historical information and totally unnecessary to your well-being. For one so young, Leah, you've had a lot dumped on you in your life. I didn't want to be one more bad thing."

"Will you be honest with me from now on?" Leah asked. "Will you tell me exactly what's going on? Exactly what your doctor says?"

"Yes," Neil said. "No need to shelter you anymore. From now on out, the whole truth, and nothing but the truth, so help me God."

Leah managed a smile for him. *The truth.* She hoped they *all* could handle it.

Later that night, Leah composed a letter to Ethan. After telling him about Neil's previous cancer diagnosis, she poured out her feelings:

Weird, isn't it? That Neil and I should have so much in common without me knowing about it until now. I don't think it's right that he and Mom kept the truth from me, but it's been done and I know I shouldn't hold it against them. I believe Neil really thought he was doing the best thing for me. But it would have been good for me to know that he'd been through chemo before I started. I was pretty scared about it, and he could have helped me.

I worry about Mom getting through this too. She's not exactly a rock. Neil doesn't want us to worry. He wants us to go on with our lives. But how am I supposed to concentrate every day in school, wondering if he really does have cancer again?

I miss you, Ethan. I wish I could see you and talk to you. You always cheered me up whenever I felt down this summer. I still think about summer, you know. I still remember our being together, and your trying out English things. How are things going with your family? I know you miss Rebekah. I know I do. But

*whenever I start to miss her big-time, I
think about the day of her funeral and
what I saw in the woods. That always
makes me feel better.*

*In your last letter, you asked me how
my doctor's appointment went in Septem-
ber. Dr. Thomas says I'm doing just fine
and that my MRI and X rays look clear.*

Leah stopped writing and leaned back in
her desk chair. The house was eerily quiet.
Outside her window, the night looked
black and deep. Her windowpane felt cool.
Leah shivered. She reread what she'd written and shivered again. Her X rays looked
clear and she didn't have to go back in for a
checkup until spring. Yet a hard, cold knot
had settled in her stomach. She couldn't
seem to get rid of it. Yes, it was true that
things looked good for her medically. But
then Neil had thought the same thing. He'd
thought he was perfectly fine. And now he
was sick again.

Leah didn't want anything to happen to
Neil. He'd been good to her mother, good
to Leah. He was different from the other

stepfathers she'd had. He was kind, generous. Neil *had* to get well. She and her mother needed him.

Leah buried her face in her hands and wept.

THREE

"Hey, Leah! Wait up!"

Leah turned to see Sherry Prater, a girl from her English class, coming toward her down the hall. While they weren't exactly best buddies, Sherry was friendly and energetic, and Leah liked her. Sherry was overweight, and therefore not on the social A-list. This suited Leah just fine. Leah had been with the in crowd at her former high school and thought the distinction highly overrated. "What's up?" she asked the out-of-breath Sherry.

"I was wondering if you were going to the football game Friday night. I thought we might hook up and sit together."

"I forgot about the game."

Sherry stared at Leah as if she were speaking a foreign language. "This game's against Henderson. They're our biggest rival! Everybody's going."

"My stepfather's not well," Leah said. "He's in the hospital." In fact, Neil had been in the hospital for the better part of the week.

"I didn't know." Sherry's brown eyes filled with concern. "Is he going to be all right?"

"I don't know yet. He's going through some tests."

"That's too bad. When you find out what's wrong, will you tell me?"

Leah agreed. "As for the game, I'll let you know if I decide to go."

Sherry looked pleased. "It's not just because everybody's going that I want to go," she confided. "It's because of Dave Simmons." Her eyes took on a soft look. "I think he's so gorgeous."

Dave was Johnson High's primary football star. Leah thought him conceited, vain and even cruel. One boy had been sent to the hospital after Dave had crushed him during a game. The next day, Dave had bragged about it. "You really like him?" Leah asked.

Sherry nodded. "Of course, he'll never notice me, but it's nice to dream."

"I know what you mean," Leah said, thinking of Ethan.

"You've got a guy?"

"He doesn't live around here."

"A long-distance romance . . ."

Leah chuckled over Sherry's dreamy expression. "Actually, he's Amish."

Sherry's jaw dropped. "Are you kidding? The Amish keep to themselves. How'd you even find each other?"

"It's a long story." Leah realized she'd said more than she'd meant to. "Listen, I've got to run." She waved goodbye and hurried out to her car in the student parking lot. The October air smelled crisp and clean, and the sky was a brilliant blue. Yet she felt sad and lonely. Mentioning Ethan had only made her miss him more. She had no idea when she'd see him again. Still, he had promised he would come see her. And Ethan always kept his word. Right now, his promise was the only bright spot in her life.

————

When Leah got to Neil's hospital room, her mother was there, as was Neil's oncologist, Dr. Nguyen. She was a young, petite Asian woman with black hair held against the nape of her neck by an eye-catching silver barrette.

Neil said, "Doctor, this is my daughter, Leah."

His introduction surprised Leah. He'd called her his daughter.

Dr. Nguyen smiled an acknowledgment. "I've just been going over your father's test results."

Leah caught Neil's eye. The transition had been made. Without ceremony, she'd officially passed from "step" into daughter status. She wasn't sure how she felt about it. At the moment, she didn't have time to dwell on it, because Dr. Nguyen was continuing to talk.

"There is evidence of cancer in your liver, Mr. Dutton."

The words fell like heavy weights. Leah's mother cried, "No!" Leah felt sick to her stomach.

"Everything points to it—abdominal bloating, the tenderness in that area when I examined you, your jaundice, plus the radioisotope scan and the needle biopsy. The pathologist's report shows a clear grouping of cancerous cells."

"I don't believe it!" Leah's mother blurted out.

"I wouldn't make this up, Mrs. Dutton," the doctor said.

Neil took his wife's hand. "It'll be all right, Roberta."

Leah saw tears fill her mother's eyes and her knuckles grow white as she gripped the bed rail. Her mother said, "But they took out his bad kidney years ago. How could he have cancer in his liver now?"

"Some maverick cells escaped surgery and chemo. It happens. The cells get into the bloodstream, travel down the portal vein and metastasize in the liver. They can lie dormant, then activate."

Neil cleared his throat. "All right. That's the worst of it. What are we going to do about it?"

"Chemotherapy is the standard treatment procedure."

Neil winced. "It didn't work before. How about radiation?"

"Unfortunately, radiation is very destructive to liver cells and not very harmful to liver cancer cells."

"What about surgery?" Leah's mother asked.

"Not an option in Neil's case."

"I hate chemo," Neil said sullenly.

Dr. Nguyen put her hand on Neil's arm. "We *have* made improvements in the drugs since you went through it before. The side effects can be much less horrific. I'm going to do a minor surgical procedure to insert a shunt into your abdomen. You'll wear an infusion pump and the chemo will be administered automatically, in small amounts, twenty-four hours a day."

"When do I start?"

"I want to begin treatment at once."

"Will it work this time?" Roberta's question sounded hostile and accusatory, as if Dr. Nguyen was somehow to blame for Neil's diagnosis.

"Second chemo protocols aren't always as successful as the first," Dr. Nguyen said cautiously. "But it's still your best hope."

Leah let her words sink in. By the time

she grasped the full meaning, Dr. Nguyen was talking again. "I'm scheduling you for surgery tomorrow morning. I'll get the shunt in and get you regulated. You should be headed home in a couple of days."

"Then what?"

"Then we wait it out, keep testing you for progress and see what happens."

Leah, Neil and her mother all looked into each other's eyes. No one asked the obvious: *"What happens if it doesn't work?"*

Leah went home alone, leaving her mother and Neil to have dinner together in his hospital room. They had asked her to stay, but she excused herself, saying she had homework. In truth, she couldn't stand hanging around the hospital one more minute.

At home, she brought in the mail and found a letter from Ethan. Eagerly she tore open the envelope.

Dear Leah,
    I just got your letter and am writing you right away. I am sick inside my heart about your stepfather's illness. I have also

told Charity and together we will pray for him. And for you and your mother.

I also miss you, Leah. I, too, think of our summer with each other. Your smile is always before me, inside my mind, making my heart glad. On weekends, I still dress English and go into town to be with my friends. Except it is not nearly so much fun as when you lived in town. I pass by the apartment building where you lived and I want to run up and pound on the door and have you open it and let me inside. But you are not here, no matter how hard I wish for it.

We miss Rebekah very much. Ma cries sometimes when she thinks no one sees her. She and Oma and Charity go to the cemetery some afternoons, just to be with Rebekah, even though we know her spirit is with God and only her body lies under the ground.

I fear that Pa and I are not getting along very well. He wants me to return to church and stop running with "that wild bunch" (as he calls my friends). I tell him over and over that I am not yet ready, but it only makes him angry. It is *good that we have so much work to do on the farm to prepare for winter. Hard work keeps us too tired to argue.*

Sarah had her baby—a little boy they named Josiah Christian. He is very handsome. I like being an uncle. When he grows up, I will tell him of his aunt Rebekah. She would have loved him. Like a little doll.

I must close now, for it is late and my lamp is burning low. Thank you for your letters, Leah. They make my days happier. I keep the picture of you in my pocket, next to my heart.

Ethan

P.S. Charity says that I am to tell you hello. Hello.

Leah finished reading the letter through tear-filled eyes. The ache within her was so real she was certain it would ooze through her skin and onto the paper. She reread the letter, then pressed it against her cheek, imagining the paper in Ethan's hands, touching his skin.

Leah had returned from the summer believing that with Rebekah's death, the worst was over, that there was no place to go but up. But now Neil had been diagnosed with liver cancer and her mother was falling apart. Leah and Ethan were miles away from each other. She still had to face future checkups for her own health—which, she now realized, was a total unknown.

What about me? Leah wondered. Will I get sick again too?

Like Neil, Leah had convinced herself that cancer was behind her—that either Gabriella had made it disappear or the chemo treatments had succeeded. Like Neil, Leah thought she was home free. But Neil's cancer had returned like an evil ghost. And now he had to begin his fight against it all over again.

Leah vowed to help him however she could. They were comrades in a battle against a mutual enemy. She'd lost her real father without ever knowing him. She didn't want to lose this one.

FOUR

Leah didn't think twice. The next morning, the day of Neil's minor surgery, she missed school and sat with her mother in the waiting area. She wished the two of them could be anyplace else. "He'll be fine," Roberta insisted. "Neil has the constitution of a much younger man. This won't keep him down for long." Her mother's forced cheerfulness got on Leah's nerves. Roberta was the picture of health. She didn't know what it felt like to be shattered by the three words *You have cancer.*

"I just want him to be okay," Leah said with emotion. "It isn't fair he has to go through this twice."

"No, it isn't," her mother agreed. "But then, when has it ever been fair?"

Neil needed several more days in the hospital after the surgery, but by the end of the week he was sent home to recuperate. He wore sensors, wires, and tubing that controlled the constant flow of chemotherapy drugs into his body. A special belt around his waist held a small black monitoring device that resembled an overgrown pager. It beeped if a line clogged.

"How's your stepfather doing?" Sherry asked Leah after school a few weeks later. They were putting their books in their lockers.

"He's hanging in there. He sleeps a lot, and he's sick to his stomach, but his doctor says he'll gradually adjust and then he'll feel better."

"It's so awful that he's got cancer. It's such a scary disease."

Leah thought, *You don't know the half of it,* but said, "Neil can handle it."

"Are you going to the Harvest Ball?" Sherry changed the subject. Next to the prom, the Harvest Ball was the biggest event of the high-school year.

"I don't think so." Leah shut her locker and twirled the combination lock. "I really don't want to."

"Is it because of that guy you told me about? The Amish one?"

"Even if Ethan weren't in my life, there's still nobody I'd like to go with." Leah had gotten only two more letters from Ethan. She made excuses for him to herself—that he was busy with farmwork and exhausted by day's end—but she couldn't get Martha Dewberry out of her mind. Martha had all but told Leah last summer that once she was out of the picture, Ethan would come back to Martha, the Amish girl his parents wanted him to marry. Leah hoped it wasn't true, but she and Ethan were so far apart and weren't getting any closer.

"I'd give anything to be asked," Sherry said with a sigh.

"Maybe someone will ask you."

"Right. And maybe there really is a Santa Claus."

"Stop putting yourself down. You're a great person, Sherry. A guy would be lucky to go out with you."

"If only boys thought like girls instead of boys," Sherry said. "I know I'm not pretty." She gave Leah a wistful smile. "Anyway, it's nice of you to say that, Leah."

By the time Leah got to the parking lot, most of the cars were gone. Her red convertible sat by itself in the sunlight. She was about to get inside when she heard someone call her name. She turned to see Dave Simmons coming toward her.

"Wait a minute," he said. "I've been waiting for you."

Leah saw Dave's car sitting near the back of the parking lot. Several of his football buddies were lounging against it. "What is it?" she asked.

Dave's neck was as thick as a bull's, his hands as large as ham hocks. His head was shaved except for a brown tuft on top. Because of his sheer size, he reminded Leah of Jonah Dewberry, Ethan's friend whom she hadn't liked too much.

Dave glanced over at his friends. "I want to ask you to the Harvest Ball."

Leah stared at him blankly.

"You haven't been asked yet, have you?"

Leah shook her head, trying to assemble her thoughts. "I hadn't planned on going," she finally said.

Dave grinned. "Then plan on going with me."

He tossed another look toward his friends, which irritated Leah. "Thanks, but no thanks."

He stared at her as if he hadn't heard correctly. "But I want to take you."

Looking at this boy brought back memories of Ethan, of his gentleness and his quiet, unassuming manner. Dave figured every girl in the school was dying to be noticed by him, and it irked her. "Look, if you want to ask somebody, ask Sherry Prater."

"Who?"

"Sherry. You must know her. The girl whose locker's next to mine."

"That cow?" Dave shook his head. "No way."

Leah saw red. "She's a nice person, and you have no right to call her names." She jerked open her car door and swung into the seat.

"Hey!" Dave looked startled. "I asked *you* to go to the dance with me."

"Not if you were the last person on earth." Leah threw the car into gear and drove out of the parking lot, leaving Dave Simmons standing on the asphalt.

Leah's rejection of Dave's offer became the talk of the school. Even Sherry asked, "Why did you say no? I can't believe it. Was it because you knew I liked him?"

"He's not my type." Leah vowed she'd never tell Sherry what Dave had said about her.

"Well, I'd give anything if he'd asked me. Course, we both know he never would."

"Don't waste yourself," Leah said. "You're too good for him."

"A girl can wish, can't she?" Sherry asked.

"Sure," Leah said with a shrug. "Dreaming's free." She dreamed about Ethan, but dreaming hadn't brought him any closer. And she had once dreamed of belonging to a nice little family, but with Neil's illness, that dream was caving in on her too.

Over the next few weeks, Neil slowly rallied as he adjusted to his chemo dose. It was

mid-November when he asked Leah,
"Would you walk with me out to the
barn?"

"Sure." The refurbished barn was where
Neil kept his collection of antique automobiles. He had once enjoyed polishing them,
tuning up their already perfect engines, and
sometimes taking Leah and her mother out
for a drive in the countryside. But his medical ordeal had kept him preoccupied and
away from the old machines.

When they reached the barn, Leah slid
open the door and turned on the light.
Large tarpaulin-covered mounds peppered
the clean cement floor. How different this
barn was from the one on Ethan's farm,
where the smell of hay and livestock filled
the air.

Neil walked over to one of the hulking
mounds and peeled back the cover to reveal
a shiny maroon-and-chrome hood. He patted the metal surface as if it were a pet.
"I've collected these cars all my life. They're
worth a great deal of money. I've been
thinking that maybe it's time to start selling
them."

"You can't do that," Leah declared,

alarmed by the resignation in Neil's voice. "You love these cars. Who'll take care of them the way you have?"

"Any number of enthusiasts," Neil said.

"Well, I think it's a bad idea. You're going to regret it if you do."

"I can't keep them up the way they should be kept," Neil said sadly. "I feel lousy."

"I could help you," Leah offered.

Neil smiled at her. "You don't know a crankcase from a tire iron."

"I could learn."

"I wouldn't ask that of you, Leah. No, you're young and you should be dating and having fun. High school is fun for you, isn't it?"

Leah shrugged.

"You ever think about what you want to do after high school? How about college? You make good grades. How'd you do on those SATs?"

"My scores aren't in yet," Leah said. If the truth were known, Leah had no burning desire to go to college. She'd never been interested in any particular subject in school and figured that without some purpose for going, college would just be a waste of time. She said, "Maybe I'll just get a job when I graduate."

"You could take a job aptitude test. We gave them all the time when I worked in Detroit. It helped us fit the applicant to a job. It might help you define your goals."

This was more than she wanted to think about right then. "Maybe later," she said evasively. "I don't like talking about the future very much."

Neil studied her kindly. "Is that because you're afraid that what's happened to me could happen to you?"

With uncanny insight, Neil had looked inside her and uncovered her deepest, most nagging fear. "Maybe."

"Just because my cancer returned doesn't mean yours will, Leah. You can't equate the two. Besides, let's not forget your mysterious friend, Gabriella. She played an important role in your recovery."

Aside from Ethan and Charity, only Neil had believed that something supernatural had happened to Leah through the mysterious Gabriella. "I don't know what to believe anymore," Leah said. "If Gabriella really cared about me, where is she now? You could sure use a little divine intervention."

"God doesn't owe people miracles, Leah."

"Well, I don't think it's fair. You'd think God would be nicer to the people who believe in him. You'd think he'd show some pity."

"Fortunately, God doesn't play favorites. If he did, we'd all be striving to earn his attention, just to get the perks."

Leah had no rebuttal. She turned her attention back to the cars. "Please don't sell all your cars, okay? I'll help you take care of them, but please don't sell them."

Neil rubbed his temples wearily. His skin had suddenly taken on a sickly gray pallor. "I guess I could hang on to them for a while longer. Maybe I won't always feel this crummy." He took her arm. "Will you walk me back to the house? I'm feeling a little woozy."

Leah let Neil lean against her, and together they returned to the house.

FIVE

Right before Thanksgiving, Dr. Nguyen said that there was evidence that Neil's cancer was responding to treatment. Neil was feeling better too, and to celebrate, he took Leah and Roberta into Chicago for holiday shopping and the theater. Leah loved the hotel Neil chose, especially since she had a lavish room all to herself. Her window looked out onto State Street, where Christmas decorations sparkled and glittered from lampposts, and colorful storefronts with animated displays attracted throngs of tourists.

The three of them ate Thanksgiving dinner, with turkey and all the trimmings, in an elegant restaurant. On Friday, while Neil rested, Leah and her mother went Christmas shopping. On Saturday, her mother took her into a photographer's studio. "I thought we could give Neil a picture of us together for Christmas," she told Leah.

A makeup artist and hairstylist prepared them for the shoot, which took hours. But Leah enjoyed the session, and when they headed back to the hotel, she told her mother it had been a good idea.

"I want Neil to be happy," her mother responded. "He's kind and loving, and I . . . I . . ." Her voice broke.

Leah studied her with some surprise. Lately she had not given much thought to the way Neil's illness was affecting her mother. Suddenly Leah saw that in spite of her mother's apparent cheerfulness, it had all been a terrible strain on her. "He's got good doctors," Leah offered awkwardly.

"You and Neil are all I have," her mother said. "You're all I want to have."

Was her mother concerned about her, too? She usually acted as if Leah's diagnosis had been some huge mistake, some medical blunder. But now, with Neil's health in doubt, she seemed much more frightened. "Don't worry," Leah said as casually as she could. "We'll both be fine."

Her mother reached over and squeezed Leah's hand, and Leah was amazed at how comforted she felt by this simple act.

On Sunday they drove home, the car and its trunk stuffed with gifts and goodies. Leah's mother chattered all the way. Neil nodded and mumbled "Hummm" a lot, and Leah stared out at the brown and dreary countryside, thinking. Here she was, seventeen years old, and for the first time in her life she felt like a member of a family— the kind of family portrayed on TV and in magazine stories. All the holidays of her past stretched behind her like a road paved with half-formed bricks. She'd never had a stepfather like Neil. The others had been imitations, men who had been indifferent to her—or worse, overly friendly. None of them had showed her the kindness and acceptance that Neil had.

But Leah couldn't help wondering what it would have been like if her real father had stayed with her and her mother. Would he have been the kind of father Neil was to her? She would never know. All she knew was that she wanted Neil to be well. Like her mother, she wanted him around for a long, long time.

Two weeks before Christmas break, Leah was hurrying down the hall at school, not looking where she was going, when she ran smack into Dave Simmons.

"Whoa," he said as she jumped back, dazed. "Is there a fire drill?"

"Sorry," Leah said. Ever since their encounter in the parking lot, they'd given each other a wide berth. She bent to pick up the books she'd dropped.

Dave crouched next to her. "You know, with football season over, I have more time for hanging around. I thought I'd give you another chance to date me."

Leah arched an eyebrow and asked, "You're joking, aren't you?"

His eyes did look amused, and he wore a half grin. "Maybe a little." He stood and hauled her to her feet. "I'd like to start over, though. So how about we go out Saturday night?"

"It's nothing personal," Leah said, telling him a half-truth, "but I really don't want to."

Dave looked incredulous. "You already have a guy? Is that it?"

"Yes. He doesn't live around here, though."

Dave's eyes narrowed. "It seems to me like you're wasting your time, then. If he's not around, why not date someone else? He probably is."

"I'd rather not."

Dave shook his head and smirked. "Suit yourself. But this is your last chance with me."

"Thanks for the warning." Leah heaved her books onto her hip and hurried off to class just as the bell rang.

She couldn't concentrate the whole hour. Not only was she angry about Dave's arrogance, but she was also worried. What if Dave was right? Leah knew how tight the group of Amish kids was. Certainly Ethan was around Martha every weekend.

Letters weren't cutting it anymore. Leah wanted to see Ethan. She wanted him to hold her and say the things he'd written in his letters to her face. A plan began to form. With Christmas break coming, maybe she could drive up to Nappanee and visit him. Even a few hours with him would be better than nothing. And what if she went and stayed the week after Christmas? *But where?* She couldn't stay with Ethan's family at the farm. Mr. Longacre had never made a secret of his feelings toward Leah's friendship with Ethan. Then she remembered Kathy, the girl she'd worked with at the inn all summer. Would Kathy let Leah stay with her?

It took Leah two days to screw up her courage, but on Saturday she called Kathy and casually outlined her plan. She was rewarded by Kathy's enthusiastic endorsement of the idea. Kathy thought it "so romantic" and assured Leah that she'd be welcome.

Leah told her mother about Kathy's invitation, choosing her words carefully. Surprisingly, she met with little resistance. "Neil and I are going to Detroit a few days after Christmas," her mother said. "Some of his old friends are throwing a huge party New Year's Eve. You're welcome to come

along, but if you'd rather do something
with your friends, that's all right."

Leah sat down and wrote Ethan, mailed
the letter, and spent several days nervously
awaiting his reply. What if he wrote her not
to come? Then what would she do?

Three days before Christmas, Ethan's reply arrived in the mail. Clutching the letter,
Leah threw herself on the living room sofa
and tore it open.

Dear Leah,

*I could not believe my eyes when I
read your letter. You are coming. I will
see you face to face. I cannot tell you how
this news makes my heart happy! I have
been thinking of many ways that I could
come see you. Now you will be here and
we will be together.*

*Leah, I have much to tell you. Papa
and I have harsh words almost every day.
This makes Ma cry. Charity, Elizabeth,
and even Oma cry too. I do not like to
make my family unhappy. I am very
mixed up. I do not know who I am anymore. I do not know where I belong.*

But this is not what I want to say now.

I will talk to you when you come after Christmas. I think of last Christmas. You were in the hospital—not a happy time for you, but a happy time for me because I met you. Leah, have a good Christmas, then come and see me. I will be waiting.

Ethan

Thoughtfully Leah folded the letter. What did he mean by "I do not know who I am"? This didn't sound like Ethan at all. For her, Christmas couldn't come and go fast enough.

On Christmas morning, Leah handed out presents to Neil and her mother from the mountain of gifts heaped beneath the ornately decorated tree in the living room. Leah's favorite gift was a gold charm bracelet from Neil. "Oh my gosh!" she cried, trying it on. "This is so gorgeous! Thank you."

Neil looked pleased. "I picked it out myself. I chose a few charms, but there's plenty of room for more. I think the idea is to add one every time something significant happens in your life."

"Like little milestones," her mother said.

"Charm bracelets are very fashionable, you know."

Leah examined each tiny charm. There was a silhouette of the state of Indiana, replicas of a vintage car and an Amish buggy, and a charm symbolizing Chicago—for the vacation they'd had there together. But the charm that made a lump rise in Leah's throat was an angel. The angel's face was a diamond chip. Leah locked eyes with Neil. He offered a knowing smile. "So you'll always have an angel with you," he said.

Leah jumped to her feet. "This one's yours. We saved it for last." She dragged a large, square object from behind the living room curtain and set it in front of Neil.

Neil tore off the paper to discover a framed photograph of his wife and Leah. "Beautiful," he said. "Absolutely beautiful. Thank you."

Leah's mother bent down and pulled another box from beneath her chair. "This goes with it."

The box held a photo album, and every page held pictures of them, some from the recent photo session. Leah looked over Neil's shoulder as he thumbed through it.

"I'm the luckiest man in the world," he said. "And I have two of the most beautiful women in the world to prove it."

Leah fingered the charm bracelet and held it up. The diamond-faced angel caught the lights from the tree and winked at her. Leah wondered if Gabriella might be watching—and feeling pleased.

Leah was ready to go early the next after-noon for Nappanee. The day was cold, the skies cloudy, but there was no snow in the forecast. "You drive carefully," her mother told her. "And call us the minute you get to Kathy's house."

"You and Neil have fun in Detroit," Leah said. "See you on New Year's Day."

When Leah arrived in Nappanee at dusk, she drove down familiar streets. The front of the inn where she'd worked resem-bled a picture on a Victorian Christmas card. As she pulled into Kathy's driveway, Kathy came out to meet her.

"Leah, you look great!" Kathy said. The dark-haired girl was bundled in jeans and a bright red sweater. Little Christmas tree earrings dangled from her ears.

"You do, too," Leah said, hauling her duffel bag from the car.

Leah followed Kathy inside and up to her bedroom. She tossed her bag onto a cot cluttered with stuffed animals.

"Remember this?" Kathy held up a picture of Leah and herself. They were standing in front of the inn in their uniforms, holding up mops and brooms.

"I forgot these were taken. Boy, those were ugly uniforms."

Kathy laughed. "I'm working there again this summer. How about you?"

"Who knows?" Leah said with a shrug.

"Only six more months of high school, then I'm off to college. I can't wait."

"I'm not sure what I'll be doing yet. Where are you going?"

"Boston College. I want to study physical therapy."

There was a knock on the bedroom door, and one of Kathy's sisters stuck her head inside. "Leah, there's someone at the front door for you. It's a boy."

"Go, girl!" Kathy said, giving Leah a shove.

Leah hurried down the stairs. The foyer was empty.

"He's on the porch," Kathy's sister whispered. "He wouldn't come in."

Leah opened the door. A blast of cold air struck her face. Ethan was standing in a pool of light. "Hello, Leah," he said. Leah flung herself into his open arms.

Six

Ethan cradled Leah's face between his palms and said, "You are as beautiful to me as ever."

Just looking up into his blue eyes made Leah's knees go weak. "Oh, Ethan. . . . I've missed you so much."

His lips found hers. The warmth of his mouth broke through the icy chill of the night air. His kiss lingered; then he hugged her hard against his chest. He was dressed English. Even through the layers of coat and sweaters he wore, she felt his heart thudding. He smelled clean like soap and tasted of cinnamon candy. She wrapped her arms around him tightly.

"I could not wait until the morning to see you," he said. "I had to come tonight."

"How did you get here?" Leah peered around him, half expecting to see his Amish buggy and his horse, Bud. What she saw was Jonah's old beat-up green car.

"I have learned to drive," Ethan said. "I have my license now."

Leah was shocked. "You never told me that in your letters."

"I wanted to surprise you."

"What's your father say about it?"

"He does not know."

This wasn't typical of the Ethan she knew. The old Ethan never would have gone against his father's wishes or acted behind his father's back. "Do you like driving?"

"Yes. And getting places takes less time. I like that too."

"But you still live at home?"

"Only during the week. On weekends I stay in town at Jonah's. He has a job in town now. And his own apartment. Many new friends, too. It is often like one big party."

Leah realized that many changes had oc-

curred in the few months she and Ethan
had been apart. "Jonah always told me he'd
stay Amish, that English ways were for
fling-taking only."

"He is still Amish. We are all Amish."
Ethan sounded defensive. "Trying out
English ways will not change who we
are."

"How does Charity feel about Jonah living on his own? Does she come to his parties?" Ethan's sister had once confided to
Leah that she expected one day to marry
Jonah.

"She has come to a few parties, but before Christmas she told Jonah she would
not see him again unless he changed his
habits and came back to the Amish way."

"I'll bet he didn't take that too well."

"He got very drunk. And very sick."
Ethan smoothed Leah's hair. "I do not
want to talk about Jonah and Charity. I
want to talk about us."

"What about us?"

"You will be here only a week, and I
want to spend all of my time with you."

"What about your farm chores?"

"The heavy work is done until spring.

Simeon is expected to take on more of the easier work I have been doing. I have thought about getting a job in town for the winter."

Leah stepped back. "Can you do that?"

"It is something we Amish often do during the wintertime to earn extra money."

"What would you do? What can you do?"

Ethan's eyes took on a mischievous sparkle. "Do you think I have no talents except pitching hay and mending fences?"

Leah felt her face redden. Ethan had gone to school only through the eighth grade, and she wasn't sure what kind of job skills he possessed. "Of course not. I was just wondering, that's all."

"I am a good carpenter. And there are Amish farmers who have no sons or who do not stay with the old ways. They have machinery to make jobs easier. I can work at one of these farms."

"Is this what you want?"

"What I want," Ethan said quietly, "is to spend every minute of this week with you. I will be staying at Jonah's here in town all week long so that we can be together."

She tightened her arms around his waist again. "All right. But I want to see Charity, too. Is it okay if I go out to your farm?"

"Certainly it is all right."

"Then I'll go in the morning."

"I will go with you," he said. He gave her Jonah's address. "Come and get me when you are ready."

He kissed her goodnight. Leah watched him return to Jonah's old car and drive away. She felt unsettled. She was so out of step with Ethan's life. When she'd left in August, he had been testing the limits of his Amish upbringing—but just slightly. Now, only a few months later, he was driving and talking of taking a job. Ethan hadn't been kidding when he'd written, "I do not know where I belong."

Leah was up early the next morning and ate breakfast with Kathy and her sisters. Once their parents had headed off to work, Leah drove over to Jonah's apartment. Kathy was very understanding. Leah was grateful that she could just go and be with Ethan.

Ethan opened the door at her first knock.

"Good morning, Leah!" His smile lit up his face.

Kissing him lightly, Leah stepped into a living room area littered with newspapers, magazines, videotapes and old pizza boxes. Pillows were scattered on the floor, and plastic cups, some half filled, dotted the tops of a coffee table and two lamp tables. "Boy," she said. "Your livestock lives better than this."

Ethan laughed. "We are not very tidy. The others are at work now. There will be a party tomorrow night. Come and meet them."

Leah had gone to Amish parties before and had felt like an outsider. "Will I be the only English?"

"No. I have told you, Jonah has many new friends. Most are English."

"But will any of your Amish friends be here?" Leah was thinking specifically about Jonah's sister, Martha.

Ethan nodded. "We Amish still do many things together. We have been friends a long time. Jonah invites everyone, but not everyone comes."

Leah felt sure that Martha would show

up, but she decided not to let the thought upset her. After all, Ethan had made it quite clear that it was Leah he wanted to be with all week.

The drive out to the farm along the flat, familiar country road brought memories of summer back to Leah. The fields had been green, a sea of cornstalks. Now the corn had been harvested and the stalks were brown, dry and broken. Patches of snow dotted the roadside, and puddles of water were iced over.

Leah came to the fence that marked the boundary of the Longacre farm and slowed down. She could hardly stand to look upon the place where a truck had plowed into the produce stand, flattening the fence behind it and killing Rebekah, who had been in its path. "The fence looks as if it was never hit," Leah said.

"It does not take wood long to weather," Ethan said.

Or for little girls to die, Leah thought. The pain of Rebekah's death struck her hard and deep. She could only imagine what it must feel like for Ethan to pass this place every day.

Ethan peered through the windshield at the gray sky. "We will have snow by midmorning."

"You can tell that just by looking at the sky?"

"I have been reading the signs of coming weather all my life. The winter will be hard this year."

"How do you know?"

"The woolly caterpillars grew extra-thick coats last fall. When they do, winter will be very cold."

"Gee . . . and all this time I've been watching the Weather Channel."

Ethan gave her a puzzled look, then slowly smiled. "You are making a joke. I understand because I've seen this Weather Channel on Jonah's TV."

Leah returned his smile. There had been a time when Ethan hadn't caught on to her humor, because it was English. She said, "You really are different these days."

"Only in some ways," he told her.

Leah turned into the long, rutted driveway to the house. Except for the colors of winter, the old farmhouse was exactly as Leah had remembered it. The weathered

60 Lurlene McDaniel

wooden roof and siding looked stark against the sky, much as she believed they had a hundred years before when first built. No electrical or telephone wires tethered them to the present. One shutter had come off its hinge.

"I must fix that," Ethan said. "For Ma." His expression looked brooding.

Leah parked and shut off the engine, half expecting Rebekah to come flying out the door to meet them. The door swung open and instead Charity stepped onto the porch. She wore a long black Amish dress and a prayer cap. A woolen shawl was tied around her shoulders. "Leah!" she cried, hurrying to the car.

Leah got out and embraced her friend. "Surprise! I couldn't stay away."

Charity glanced at her brother, and Leah could have sworn she saw a shadow of sadness flicker across Charity's eyes. The look vanished as Charity grabbed Leah's hand. "Come inside where it is warm. I have tea and fresh bread made."

Inside the kitchen, Leah felt the warmth from the old woodstove in the corner. The room smelled like baking bread and warm apples. Tillie Longacre, Charity and Ethan's mother, greeted Leah, asked a few polite questions, then cut some warm bread, placed it on a plate, and carried it out of the room.

"Oma has a bad cold," Charity explained as she poured Leah hot tea, "so Mama is taking her a snack."

"I hope she'll be okay," Leah said. Oma had sometimes reminded Leah of her Grandma Hall.

"I will look in on her," Ethan said.

When Leah was alone with Charity, she asked, "How are you doing?"

Charity sighed. "Winters are very long. I miss Rebekah very much."

"So do I."

"But Sarah's new baby is precious." Charity brightened. "I spend many afternoons at Sarah's helping with little Josiah. He is most adorable."

"Listen, Ethan told me about you and Jonah." Leah changed the subject, not knowing how long the two of them would be alone. "I'm sorry. I know you liked him."

"I still like him, but I cannot be with him when he is so wild. Until he returns to the community and Amish ways, I will have nothing to do with him."

Charity looked sad. Leah wondered how much of Charity's decision was hers and how much of it was her family's. "I'm sure Jonah will come around," Leah said. "He always told me that he would have his fling and return to Amish ways."

"He did?"

"Well, yes—" Leah got no further. The outside door opened and Mr. Longacre stepped into the room. His expression looked grim. He took one look at Leah and walked straight past her without saying a word.

SEVEN

Charity rose from her chair, looking shocked, then turned toward Leah. "I-I'm sure Papa was in a hurry," she stammered.

Leah felt her cheeks begin to burn. Mr. Longacre had snubbed her on purpose. "Maybe I should go."

"No, Leah. I know Papa didn't mean to offend you. Ever since Rebekah's accident . . ." Charity didn't finish the sentence. "Please, do not take offense," she said.

Before Leah could respond, Mr. Longacre swept back into the kitchen, his wife on his heels. "Hello, Leah," the man said stiffly.

"Hello, sir," Leah answered, her heart pounding. She saw Ethan slip into the room through a different door.

"I saw your car parked in my yard," Jacob said. "I thought something might have happened."

"I'm only visiting for a few days," Leah told him. "I'm staying in town with a friend."

"Would you like some tea, Jacob?" Tillie asked.

"No. I have things to do in the barn." He turned to Ethan, and the look that passed between them made Leah's stomach knot. "You will come to the barn before you leave," Mr. Longacre said. It wasn't a request.

"I will come," Ethan answered, his expression grim.

"Have a nice visit," Mr. Longacre said in Leah's general direction. In another second he was out the door, shutting it firmly behind him.

Tillie stepped forward and took Leah's hands in hers. "It is good to see you, Leah.

Rebekah spoke of you often. You were a favorite of hers."

Tears sprang into Leah's eyes. "Thank you. She was a favorite of mine, too."

"Will you have more tea?" Tillie asked, looking inside the teapot.

"No, thank you. I really should get back to town to spend some time with my friend."

"I will walk you to your car," Ethan said.

Once outside, Leah asked, "Aren't you coming with me?"

"I must go see Papa." He didn't look happy about it.

"I'll wait for you."

"No, do not wait. But before you go, walk with me into the woods." Ethan took her gloved hand in his.

Leah understood. Ethan needed to collect himself, and the woods on the back portion of the property was where he usually went to find solace. She took a deep breath. She had not been there since the day of Rebekah's funeral. But, once surrounded by the towering trees and whispering pine needles, her heart felt more at ease.

"I'm sorry I upset your father," she said.

"It is not you, Leah. It is me who displeases him."

"Because you're taking your fling?"

"I think he was certain that I had gotten over my fling by the end of last summer. I have told you how Pa does not like me to run with Jonah and his crowd."

"Or date English girls," Leah said.

"I am mixed up, Leah." Ethan turned to face her. "I have tried to care for another, but I cannot get you out of my mind. Or my heart."

Leah felt a pang of jealousy. She didn't want him to care for another. She wanted to be the only girl in his life. "I've wanted to talk to you a hundred times these past few months," she confessed. "What with Neil and all."

"Is he better?"

"He seems to be on the mend—for now. I really like Neil, Ethan. I don't know what Mom and I would do if something happened to him. Especially Mom. She and Neil get on really well together. I've never seen her happier. But this has really messed things up for all of us."

"I am sorry about all your family is going through, Leah, but you are well, and this makes me happy."

"I hope you're right."

His expression sobered. "Did you not have a good checkup when you last went for tests?" Ethan had gone with Leah to her doctor's appointment during the summer, and her mother had accompanied her to the fall appointment.

"So far, so good. But who's to say it can't all blow up in my face? Neil thought he was finished with cancer too, and look what's happened to him."

"But an angel touched you," Ethan reminded her.

"That's what you and Neil and I think, but Mom and my doctors don't believe it. Mom thinks it was a misdiagnosis, and Dr. Thomas calls it spontaneous remission. I wish I could talk to Gabriella face to face and ask her once and for all."

"You must have faith," Ethan said.

"Don't you think I'm trying to have faith? But every time I feel as if I do, something terrible happens. Rebekah dies. Neil gets sick. I just don't get it. Why do terrible things happen to nice people? Doesn't it make you mad about Rebekah?"

Ethan put his arms around Leah and rested his chin on her head. "It makes me very sad. I do not know the answers to your questions, Leah. I do not know where to go to get the answers. All my life, I grew up going to church, believing the things I was told. I accepted Amish ways, even when they did not make sense to me. Yet, today, my sister is dead and my brother Eli is gone."

The mention of his older brother made Leah pull back and study Ethan's face. He looked tormented. "Ethan, I'm sorry. Let's forget all this serious stuff and think about this whole week of being together and having fun."

He smiled. "This is a good suggestion. Right this moment, I want to think about kissing you."

Leah rose on her tiptoes. "Why think about it?"

He lowered his mouth to hers.

Around them huge, fat, wet snowflakes began to fall.

Leah left Ethan at the farm and returned to Kathy's. She found Kathy in her room, organizing her clothes closet. "I'm trying to see if my new stuff works with any of my old stuff," Kathy explained. She shut the door. "How's your boyfriend? Is the magic still there?"

"More than ever."

"Gee, Leah, liking an Amish guy is risky. They stick to their own kind."

"Not always," Leah said defensively. "Actually, Ethan's brother left the community," she confided.

Kathy didn't seem impressed. "Just watch out. Don't get hurt."

"I don't plan on getting hurt. Ethan may not know a lot about English ways, but he's the kindest, nicest guy I've ever met. The guys back home are such losers compared to him."

"But this is *his* world, Leah. How would he fit into yours? How would he get along with your regular friends? Picture him with *your* crowd."

Kathy had a point. Up until now, Leah had only been with Ethan in his hometown, in his Amish world. "In the first place, I don't hang out with any special group at my school. For that matter, I don't care to. Except for my friend Sherry, I'm not close to anyone. I'm just not interested in any of their little cliques."

"I know what you mean. Sometimes high school is just so lame. College will be my big breakout." Kathy grew thoughtful. "Still," she said, "hooking up with an Amish guy may not be the smartest thing you can do. Amish don't fit anywhere but in their small world, Leah."

"I don't care," Leah said stubbornly. "Ethan is the only guy I want in my life, period."

Kathy shrugged. "Then good luck, girl."

Ethan caught a bus to Kathy's, and after supper Leah drove the two of them back to Jonah's. Ethan was quiet, almost withdrawn, during the short drive, making Leah realize that things had not gone well between him and his father. "Do you still want to go to the party?" she asked, half wishing he'd say no.

"Yes," Ethan said. "I want us to have a

good time tonight. I want to show you off to everyone there."

The party was in full swing. Ethan headed toward the kitchen for a snack, leaving Leah alone for a moment.

From the corner of her eye, Leah saw Martha dancing with a lanky, dark-haired guy. She was dressed in tight jeans and a fitted sweater—a far cry from the Amish clothing Leah had last seen her in at Rebekah's funeral.

Martha walked over. "Ethan said you'd be coming," she said above the wail of the music. "It is good to see you."

Leah didn't believe her, but she smiled anyway and said, "It's good to be back. How have you been?"

"Busy," Martha said. "I have a job in town now. I work in a bakery selling Amish breads and making lunches for customers."

Martha sounded pleased about her independence. "Do you live in town, too?" Leah asked.

"I live at home. Jonah comes and picks me up and brings me into town to my job."

The boy Martha had been dancing with

came up beside her and slipped his arm around her waist. "Let's dance."

Leah smelled beer on his breath.

"Todd, this is Leah," Martha said. "She's Ethan's girlfriend."

Todd grinned, and Leah urged them, "Go dance." As she watched them walk away, she noticed Todd shoved his hand into the back pocket of Martha's jeans. Leah realized she'd been introduced as Ethan's girlfriend. Did that mean Martha was relinquishing her claim on Ethan?

Ethan returned with sodas. "The music is too loud. Come with me."

Leah followed him outside onto the balcony. "Leah, there is something I want to ask you," Ethan said quietly.

Instantly on alert at the tone of his voice, Leah said, "Sure, ask me anything."

"I want to see my brother Eli again. Please, will you help me find him?"

EIGHT

"Help you find Eli? What makes you think I can do that?" Ethan's request had taken Leah totally by surprise.

"You are English. You know the English world. I thought that you might know about such things."

"But I wouldn't know where to begin."

Ethan's face fell. "I am sorry. I did not know who else to ask."

Leah's heart went out to him. "Oh, Ethan, don't be sorry. I want to help you. I just don't know if I can. I mean, you've told me that Eli dropped out of sight years ago. He could be anywhere."

Ethan had confided in her the previous summer about his older brother Eli. Amish kids often quit school to help in their homes and on their farms, but Eli had wanted more education. He had attended high school, and he had won a college scholarship. Against his family's wishes, and against Amish traditions, he had left home to pursue his dreams. His leaving had forced a permanent wedge between him and his family. It had also left Ethan, who had been only ten at the time, with Eli's responsibilities. To this day, no one spoke Eli's name. To his family, it was as if Eli were dead.

"I cannot stop thinking about him." Ethan's voice sounded tormented. "I see him in my dreams—the way he was the last time I saw him. I wonder what he's doing and if he's happy. I think of how he never even knew Rebekah."

Rebekah had been born after Eli had left home. Now it was too late for them to know each other. Leah said, "Last summer, you acted as if you accepted your father's decision about Eli. What changed your mind?"

"I have been troubled about many things." Ethan shook his head sadly. "This does not seem right to me. Eli was not even a member of the church. He was never shunned, and yet he is as lost to me as Rebekah."

The Amish custom of shunning was reserved for noncompliant church members, but, according to Ethan, Eli had never been baptized, so his ejection from the Longacre household was purely the result of their father's unwillingness to allow him the freedom to be his own person.

Leah warned, "Your father won't like your contacting Eli, you know."

"I would not tell him."

"But how could you keep such a secret?"

Ethan shrugged. "I do not know. I only want to see my brother again. I do not want to think about why I should not."

Leah chewed her bottom lip thoughtfully. "I really don't know how to start searching for him. But I'll bet Neil could help. He knows everything."

The fire of hope leaped into Ethan's eyes. "Would he do such a thing? He does not even know me."

"He's never met you, that's true. But Neil would help if I asked him." Neil had been feeling good since Thanksgiving, and this type of project might be one he would be willing to take on—or at least be willing to advise her and Ethan about.

Ethan looked relieved and grateful. "Thank you, Leah. I will not forget your kindness. This has been on my mind for days, and I could not keep it inside any longer."

"No problem," Leah said, her teeth chattering. "I'm glad you told me."

Ethan slid open the glass door and a blast of heated, smoky air rushed out at them. Leah wasn't sure what was worse—freezing on the balcony or suffocating in the apartment. She stepped inside and immediately saw Jonah. He was leaning against a wall, smoking, holding a beer can and watching the dancing couples with brooding, heavy-lidded eyes.

When he caught sight of Ethan and Leah, he shoved away from the wall and sauntered over. "Hello, Leah," he said without warmth.

"Back to you," she said with more cheeriness than she felt.

"I'll get us sodas," Ethan said, and made his way toward the kitchen.

Alone with Jonah, Leah wasn't sure what to say. Jonah had never been happy about her friendship with Ethan. "Looks like this is the place to come for Amish or English," she said, trying to sound friendly.

Jonah shrugged. "My friends know they can come here whenever they like."

"And do whatever they want?"

"Yes, until the police show up. Or until the elders ban everyone from being friends with me." He sounded bitter.

"I went to see Charity yesterday," Leah said, offering the name like bait. She watched Jonah's expression harden.

"She is a silly girl—not person enough to think for herself."

"She's lonely and confused," Leah corrected. "And for reasons I can't begin to figure out, she cares about you."

Jonah took a long swig of his beer. "Well, I no longer care for her."

"Too bad. She misses you."

Jonah turned and brought his face close to Leah's. "Do not involve yourself, English. You do not know what it means to be separate."

"Separate" was how the Amish referred to themselves. They kept themselves separated from the rest of the world, following the Bible's mandate to be in the world but not of the world. Leah felt a surge of anger because Jonah had no idea where she was coming from. If he thought Amishness made a person separate, he should try having cancer. Now, *that* was separation. Leah squared her jaw. "You don't look very separate to me, Jonah. You look just like some kids I used to know in Dallas. All they did was drink and party, too. What's so separate about that?"

Jonah straightened. "If you do not like my party, Leah, then leave." He jiggled his beer can. "Empty." He crushed it in his fist. "I need a refill."

Leah watched him swagger away and felt pity for him. Jonah was caught between two ways of life. He had a foot in both, but he seemed stuck, unable to make up his mind where he wanted to stand. It scared her that Ethan might get caught in the same web of confusion.

As the week dwindled, Leah and Ethan became inseparable. Kathy's mother even invited him for dinner one night, and later Leah heard Kathy's mother tell Kathy, "What a nice boy. You should date a boy like him."

Leah heard Kathy say, "He's Amish, Mother. How many of them mingle with us in the first place?"

"Amish! I'll bet his parents are fit to be tied."

"Leah knows what she's doing," Kathy said. "She's not an idiot."

Leah was glad that Kathy had defended her, but she wasn't so sure about Kathy's conclusion. Maybe she *was* an idiot. Loving Ethan was risky. What could really ever become of it? And now that he'd asked her to help locate Eli, she felt a greater turmoil. She didn't want to let him down.

The thought of returning to school, to boring classes, was even less appealing. She could not get Neil's or her own health problems off her mind. What if Neil had a relapse? What if *she* had one? How could her mother handle both of them being sick? How could Leah turn to Ethan for support when he was hundreds of miles away? And if he lived with Jonah, would he turn into a Jonah clone? Leah could hardly stand to think about any of it.

Ethan took Leah to their favorite pizza parlor after they'd spent the afternoon ice skating. The parlor had Happy New Year banners hanging along the walls, reminding Leah that she had only two days left before she'd have to return home. She thought of Neil and her mother on their way to Detroit for the upcoming round of holiday parties with Neil's old friends.

She and Ethan both were in low moods as they nibbled halfheartedly on the food. "I don't want you to leave," Ethan said.

"And I don't want to leave," Leah confessed.

"Then don't."

She gave a mirthless laugh. "Where would I stay? In my car?"

He stared morosely out the window. "What can we do, Leah?"

Suddenly she sat up straighter. Like a bolt of lightning, an idea struck her. "You know what, Ethan? I just had the craziest idea. I can't stay here, but you can come home with me. Why don't you?"

NINE

E than asked, "Go home with you? What do you mean?"

"Just what I said. Why should you stay here? You told me you wanted to get a job. Why not get one where I live? A job's a job." Leah's excitement mounted as she tossed out possibilities.

"Where would I live?"

"With me—us," she corrected. "Me, Mom and Neil. The house is huge. Why, there's a whole other house in the basement—bedroom, bath, family room. We never even go down there. Mom hates basements." Leah waved her hand dismissively.

"We have the space, and you could live in it."

"My father would not allow—"

"You're eighteen, aren't you?" Leah interrupted him. He'd had his eighteenth birthday in October. "When you're eighteen, you don't need your father's permission. You can just leave."

"That is what Eli did." Ethan looked concerned. "It hurt Pa deeply."

"And that's another thing. If you want to find Eli, it will be easier if we look for him together. No telling where he is or how hard it's going to be to find him. But this way you can get the information more quickly because you'll be right there when Neil gets it. You won't lose days waiting for my letters."

Leah could tell that Ethan was pondering her suggestion. Having him close by her again was just what she'd dreamed about all these long months.

"What will your mother say?" Ethan asked.

Leah knew it would be a tough sell, but if Ethan was already there, it would be harder for her mother and Neil to say no. "Look, Ethan, let me worry about my family."

"I don't know, Leah." His brow puckered.

She suddenly remembered Neil's barn full of antique autos. Perhaps Ethan could help Neil maintain them. "Neil can't handle even simple chores around the house anymore. Maybe you could help out. There's lots of stuff for you to do."

Ethan nodded slowly. "Yes. I would have to help somehow."

"I'll be in school all day. And once you get a job, you'll be working, so it's not like we'd be in each other's way or anything. We'll be apart but still together." Leah shot him a broad smile.

"And if we cannot find Eli?"

"Don't give up before we even start," Leah chided.

Ethan leaned back in his chair, hooking his hands behind his head. He stared out the window for a long time. Leah's heart thudded. She knew he did nothing in haste. But the more she considered her plan, the more sense it made. They could search for

Eli without the frustration of distance between them. And she could have Ethan in her world. She had lived among the Amish. Now it was Ethan's turn to live among the English.

"When would we leave?" Ethan asked quietly.

Leah licked her dry lips. "The sooner, the better, I think. I have to start school the day after New Year's, and you need to get settled in. You know, adjusted." She didn't add that she really wanted to get home before her mom and Neil returned from Detroit. If Ethan was already moved in by the time they returned, it would be harder to throw him out. It was urgent that she get to her mother first thing, before she had time to blow a fuse.

"I want to go with you, Leah."

Ethan's simple acceptance startled her. She had expected more resistance. "Well. Okay then. You'll drive home with me. If we leave tomorrow, we can spend New Year's Eve at the house. We can watch the ball drop on TV."

He looked puzzled. "What ball?"

While she was growing up, Leah had

sometimes stayed up until midnight to watch the Times Square crowds in New York welcome in the New Year. Of course, Ethan didn't know about the yearly ritual. "I'll tell you about it on the drive home."

Ethan stood. "Come."

"Where to?"

"To go tell my parents."

Leah felt a jolt as reality hit. "Ethan, I don't know if you should tell them."

"I cannot just sneak away."

"But they may get angry and try to stop you. Maybe you could just write them after you get home with me."

"I cannot. I must tell them to their faces. And you must go with me."

She swallowed hard. "I could wait in the car. Keep the motor running."

He gave her a little smile. "No, Leah. You must be by my side. And you must tell them of your offer of a place to stay."

"But not about Eli?"

"No. That will be our secret."

Nervously Leah stood. "Are you sure you want to go tell them right now?"

"They are together tonight. It is best to go now."

With her heart thudding like thunder in her ears, Leah followed Ethan out into the cold, dark night.

Leah fought an intense internal battle as she and Ethan drove out to the farm. Now that she was about to get her way, she was scared. Was she being selfish? Would Tillie hate her? She'd come into Ethan's tidy little world and turned it on its edge. She was English, everything the Amish held in low regard. Now she was luring Ethan away from his family and the only way of life he'd known.

By the time they arrived at the farmhouse, Leah felt sick to her stomach. But she couldn't turn back now. She'd made Ethan promises, and she had to keep them.

They found his parents alone in their kitchen beside the woodstove. Jacob Longacre had the big German Bible open on his lap, and Tillie was sitting in an old rocker doing cross-stitch by the light of an oil lamp. Startled by Ethan and Leah's appearance, Jacob asked, "Has something happened?"

"Nothing bad, Pa," Ethan said. He

glanced around the shadowed room. "Where are the others?"

"Oma and Opa have retired. The children are visiting Sarah," Tillie answered.

Leah held on to the edge of the countertop, certain her knees would give way if she didn't. She saw Jacob scrutinize his son and realized that Ethan was dressed English.

Without preamble, Ethan announced to his parents, "I have decided to go away."

The room was silent except for the wood crackling in the stove.

"Where will you go?" asked his father.

"Leah has asked me to her place. I am going."

Leah expected an explosion of temper, but she was surprised. Mr. Longacre simply studied his son with resigned, contemplative eyes.

"Neil and my mother will take good care of him," Leah offered in a breathy voice.

"And who will care for his soul, Leah?" Mr. Longacre leveled a blue-eyed gaze at her.

"We're not heathens, you know. He'll be all right with us."

"Do you know for how long you will be gone?" Jacob asked, ignoring her outburst.

"I cannot say."

Jacob stood, folded his reading glasses, closed the Bible and placed it under his arm. "Do what you must do, Ethan. I cannot stop you."

"As for my work"—Ethan gestured to his surroundings—"Simeon is young and strong. He is good help. Do not let Opa work too hard."

Mr. Longacre nodded. "We will manage."

"I love you, Papa." Ethan's voice was firm.

Jacob sighed deeply. Wearily he walked over to stand in front of Ethan. Leah was close enough to see that his eyes glistened with tears. His hands were big, work-worn, covered with calluses. A lump of emotion clogged her throat.

Jacob placed his free hand on Ethan's shoulder. "And I love you, Ethan. Be careful among the English."

Jacob turned and left the room. Ethan followed his father with his gaze.

Tillie rose from her chair and set her sewing on the counter. Leah remembered summer days when they canned fruit and vegetables together, of a kitchen alive with laughter and women's voices. She saw Rebekah's sweet face reflected in Tillie's features.

Ethan reached for his mother's hand. "I will be fine, Ma."

She came closer, touched his cheek lovingly. "You are a man, my son. You must make your own way in the world. But do not forget your youth and all that we have taught you."

"I will not forget."

"Remember the words of our Lord," she said. " 'You are the salt of the earth, but if the salt loses its saltiness, how can it be made salty again? It is no longer good for anything, except to be thrown out and trampled by men.' " Tillie smiled wistfully. "It is God who calls each man whom he wants for his own. You must know if you, Ethan Longacre, have been called by God to be separate."

Tillie turned to look into Leah's eyes. "You were touched by an angel, Leah. You were blessed. But my Ethan must search his heart and discover what it is that God requires of him. Do you understand?"

Leah nodded, unable to speak.

"I will not be cut off from you, Ma," Ethan said. "I will not allow us to become strangers."

Leah heard his words as a veiled reference to Eli. She thought it extraordinary that even now, neither could speak the name aloud.

"I will always hold you in my heart," his mother said. "Just as I hold all my children there."

"I love you, Ma."

She cupped Ethan's chin. "You are my beloved son. I have lost two of my children already. I do not want to lose another."

"Ma." The word sounded strangled in Ethan's throat.

"Take good care of yourself, Ethan." Tillie picked up the oil lamp. It lit her face with an ethereal light. The ties of her prayer cap trailed to her shoulders. In her dark Amish dress, with only the lamp's light on her face, she reminded Leah of a dark ghost.

For a trembling minute, Leah thought Ethan was going to turn and tell her to go away without him, but slowly he squared his shoulders. "I must get some things from my room."

"Of course." Tillie stepped aside. Ethan bolted out of the kitchen.

Left alone with Ethan's mother, Leah almost fell apart. "I'll watch after him," she whispered hoarsely. "I promise."

"I know you will, Leah, for I know you love him too."

Leah nodded mutely, stunned by this serene woman's ability to calmly embrace whatever adversity life gave her. *So unlike my mother,* Leah thought.

In minutes Ethan was back, a homespun sack over his shoulder. "Tell Simeon and Charity and Elizabeth I am sorry I did not get to see them. Tell them I will write to them."

"I will tell them."

He took Leah's elbow and started toward the back door.

"Son," Tillie called. They turned and she held up the lamp. "Each night you are gone, I will set this in the window of your room. It will burn for you, a light to show you the way back home if you want to come."

Ethan nodded and led Leah into the night.

In the car, Leah laid her head against the headrest and allowed the bottled-up tears to flow unchecked.

TEN

Early the next morning, Leah told Kathy's family she was leaving for home. She had the perfect excuse. Bad weather had been forecast, and she thought it best to beat it home before New Year's Eve. She thanked them for allowing her to stay and gave them the small gifts she'd bought for them. She hugged Kathy good-bye, then drove straight to Jonah's, where Ethan was waiting for her.

"Is that all you're going to take?" Leah asked incredulously.

All Ethan held was a small duffel bag, a battered suitcase, and the sack he'd carried from home the night before.

"It is all I own," Ethan told her. "Too many possessions make a person prideful. And material things are not what is important in life."

"Wait till you meet my mother," Leah said, half under her breath. Leah's mother was a collector of beautiful things—clothes, furniture, jewelry.

Ethan tossed his belongings into the car and got in. He looked tired. Leah felt sorry for him. Ethan was leaving behind him all he had ever known. It was a huge step. But she was excited, too. Ethan was coming home with her. They could be together whenever they wanted.

Ethan did not sleep during the trip but stared broodingly out the window as the miles slipped away. Icy cold rain fell in globs, smacking the windshield with squishy sounds, slowing them down and making the trip twice as long as usual.

By the time Leah turned into the long driveway leading to her house, it was dark and the sleet had turned into heavy, wet snow. She pulled into the garage and exhaled with relief. "Let me turn off the security alarm." She quickly punched in the code and led Ethan inside the house. "Wow, it's cold in here."

Ethan followed her tentatively. She flipped the light switch, but nothing happened. "Oh no! The electricity's out."

"Really," Ethan said. "How will we manage?"

The silliness of the problem made Leah giggle. The Amish didn't use electricity. "Okay, I get your point. But with no electricity, there's no heat." Without power, Leah felt marooned. Outside, the winds had picked up. Driving snow pelted the house. "This blizzard could last a while," she said.

"Would that be so terrible?"

"I guess not." Her mother and Neil wouldn't be home until late on New Year's Day—or later, if the roads became impassable. Still, they wouldn't be worried about her because they thought she was at Kathy's. Two days alone with Ethan. Leah was certain she could handle it.

"Do you have a fireplace?" he asked.

"In the living room."

"Firewood?"

"In the garage."

"I will build you a fire, Leah."

She found a flashlight, several candles and a stash of matches. Ethan laid a fire in the stone hearth and lit it. Soon the flames danced and warmth seeped into the large room. Leah collected blankets, afghans and pillows and made a nest in front of the crackling fire. "Now, if we just had some food, it would be perfect," she told him.

In the kitchen they rummaged through the refrigerator and pantry and came up with hot dogs, chips, sodas and a can of baked beans. Ethan fashioned cooking sticks from wire coat hangers, and soon the aroma of cooking hot dogs filled the air. He warmed the beans deftly in a pot over the open flames.

"Who ever thought we'd have a picnic in December?" Leah asked as they ate.

"Who ever thought I'd be so far from home in December?"

"Are you all right about this, Ethan? I mean, do you wish you hadn't come with me?"

"No. I wanted to come. You would have starved without me," he teased.

"Probably." She glanced around the room. The flickering flames sent shadows dancing against the walls. The wind howled outside. "Tomorrow's New Year's Eve, but I don't think we're going to party it in."

"I will not miss the party. I am with you. That is all that matters to me."

Leah felt a tingle up her spine. "I guess we'll have to sleep here in front of the fire-place," she said, fluffing a pillow and stretching out.

"We can do as the Amish do," Ethan said. "We can bundle."

"How do we bundle?"

"It's an old Amish custom, not always approved of by parents and elders. But when dating, a boy and his girl will lie in bed together. They do not remove their clothes, but they spend the night in each other's arms."

Leah's jaw dropped. "This is an *Amish* custom?"

"Sex without marriage is forbidden," Ethan quickly added.

"I'd guess so. But—wow—doesn't bundling sort of invite trouble?"

Ethan chuckled. "Winters are long and

very cold. Amish couples do it to keep warm."

Leah rolled her eyes. If any guy but Ethan had fed her such a line, she would have laughed at him. She thought that lying in bed with a person you love all night long without going all the way would be a temptation too hard to resist. "What happens if a couple gets carried away? What if they mess around and get into trouble?" In a way, Leah found it embarrassing to discuss such ideas with Ethan, but the subject of bundling was so unexpected from the morally upright Amish, she wanted to know more.

"If a girl is with child, then they must confess their sin before the entire church and ask forgiveness."

"You mean they have to stand up in front of everybody and tell them if she gets pregnant? If that's the case, then maybe they should keep quiet and just get married."

"They usually do marry," Ethan said. "Yet they must still make a public confession."

Leah made a face. "That's awful! It sounds pretty humiliating to me."

"In God's eyes, sin is sin. It does not matter which of God's laws we break. Sinners must repent."

"Does everybody forgive them?"

"It is required to forgive."

Leah had seen how difficult it had been for Ethan's father to forgive his son Eli for leaving. "Really?" she asked.

A slow smile spread across Ethan's face. "Maybe not as quickly as it should be done," he admitted. "But that is what is supposed to happen."

Leah hugged her knees and stared into the fire. "Will your father forgive you for leaving?"

"Perhaps he already has."

"I'll be honest," Leah said, still gazing at the flames. "I felt sorry for your parents last night. And I expected your father to put up more of a fight to make you stay. Why didn't he?"

Ethan got up, threw two more logs on the fire, then returned to sit beside Leah. "He has known for a long time that I have been unhappy. We have had many talks about it. And I think that losing Rebekah wounded his heart deeply. He has said that perhaps her death was God's punishment for him."

Leah thought back to Rebekah's funeral. Even then she had disliked the stoic that's-the-way-it-is mentality of Ethan's family. She had been angry over Rebekah's sense-less death. Her discussion with Ethan at the time had brought her neither understand-ing nor comfort. "Did he mean he feels he's being punished over the way he treated Eli?"

"Yes. His heart was proud at the time. He showed Eli no mercy."

Slowly a light of understanding flickered on inside Leah's mind. "That's really why you came, isn't it? You don't just want to see Eli again because you miss him. You want to make things right between Eli and your father."

"I want to see my brother. I want to talk to him face to face. If I can persuade him to return home, even for a visit, then perhaps he and Pa can start anew."

Disappointment hit Leah hard. She had hoped that Ethan had come mostly because of what he felt for her. "Sure," she said. "I get it now."

Ethan rose on his knees, took her hands in his and forced her to look into his eyes. "I have many questions, Leah, inside my heart. Not only about Eli, but also about you and me."

Had he read her mind? She returned his gaze. The light from the fire burnished his cheek, turning his skin a warm copper color. The reflections of the flames flickered in his eyes. She could drown in those eyes. "I don't have any answers for you, Ethan."

"We will find the answers together." He traced a finger down the length of her face, sending shivers up her spine. She wanted to lie in his arms, but she was afraid. "I will not dishonor you, Leah," Ethan said. He had made the same promise to her in the summer at the campout. But now the winter winds howled, and the night was dark and long. They were alone.

"That's the problem," Leah confessed. "I don't much care about my honor right this minute."

He sat down behind her and wrapped his arms around her, nestling her back against his chest. She fit perfectly within the curve of his body. "I love you," he said into her ear. "And it is because I love you that I will do nothing to shame you."

He made her feel cherished, respected. The strength of his embrace, the warmth of the fire, the softness of the pillows and blankets covering them, combined to make Leah's eyelids grow heavy. She listened to the wail of the wind and the rhythm of Ethan's breathing. "I guess we're bundling," she murmured. "A nice custom, Ethan. I like it very much."

In the safety of Ethan's arms, Leah drifted off to sleep.

ELEVEN

By morning the storm was over and sunlight flooded the house. Ethan had kept the fire burning all night, and Leah stretched lazily, feeling warm and snuggly beneath the pile of blankets. The smell of coffee forced her eyes open. "Is the electricity back on?" she asked sleepily.

"No, but I found coffee in your kitchen and have made it for us in the fireplace."

She took a mug from him and sipped it, making a face. "This stuff always smells better than it tastes." She smiled at him shyly. "Thanks for taking care of me all night."

"A pleasure," he said with a twinkle in his eye.

She blushed, remembering the night before. She had felt comfortable in his arms, but in the clear light of the day, she was glad he had respected her enough to not take advantage of their situation. "So," she asked, "are you hungry?"

He grinned. "Are there more hot dogs?"

"We can have cereal," she said.

She wrapped the blanket around herself and padded into the kitchen. Ethan followed, and together they prepared bowls of cereal and returned to the warmth of the fire.

"I will shovel the driveway," Ethan said. "It will be clear for your mother's return."

"Once the electricity comes back on, we can do lots of things," she said. "We have a big collection of videos. And tonight is New Year's Eve."

"And we can watch the ball drop?"

She laughed. "I'll tell you all about it."

Ethan stood. "I'd better get busy. The walkway is long and the snow deep."

After he had worked an hour, Leah went

outside to join him. "Time for a break," she said. She lugged her large yellow plastic snow dish from the garage.

"But I still have much to do."

"So what? I'm bored and I think we should play."

He jammed the shovel into a snowbank. "With that?" He pointed at the bowl-shaped disk. "What is it?"

"You'll see. Come around back, where there's a hill."

The hill was at the back of the giant yard. So much snow covered it that it was hard to see exactly how steep it was. Leah tossed the dish down, lay across it on her stomach and gripped the short nylon handles on either side. "See ya!" she shouted, then scooted the disk forward. It slipped downward, picking up speed and making her squeal. At the bottom she coasted to a stop and jumped off. She trudged back up the hill and handed Ethan the dish. "Your turn."

His eyes danced. He took the disk and zipped down the hill, his laughter flowing behind him with the sprays of snow. By the time he climbed back up, she had a snowball hidden behind her back. "At home we use cardboard for such rides," he said. "And the ground is not so steep."

She tossed the snowball in his face, snatched the dish with her free hand, leaped onboard, and flew down the hill, laughing as he sputtered and wiped snow out of his eyes and mouth. "Gotcha!" she yelled.

He started down the hill after her, clomping through the snow, getting stuck in areas that were waist high, struggling against the snow's heavy wetness. Leah kept laughing. When he arrived at the bottom he doubled over, gasping for breath. "I thought you'd be in better shape," she teased, "you being a farm boy and all."

"You flirt with danger," Ethan said, lifting his gaze to hers.

"I don't think so," she needled. "You're a wimp."

He pounced on her. They rolled in the snow. Ethan stuffed handfuls of it down the front of her jacket and sweater. Leah squealed, trying in vain to fend him off. "You'll pay for this!" she promised.

He pinned her on her back, grinned and

plopped a fistful of snow in her face. "How will you make me pay?"

"I'll poison your food!" she sputtered.

"How? You don't cook without electricity."

"I'll find a way." She squirmed as he tossed another heap of snow at her face. "Get this stuff off me. It's freezing!"

He paused, looking down at her with a smile that lit up his face. "I know a good way to get the snow off." He tugged off his glove and brushed her cheeks with his bare hands. Then, holding her wrists, he bent over and kissed her with such an intensity that she was certain the snow would melt from the very heat of his mouth.

By midafternoon the electricity was back on, and Leah took a long, hot shower. Afterward she showed Ethan around the house, including the basement rooms where he would be living. He stashed his few belongings in the closet and went back upstairs with her to the kitchen.

"I have my grandmother's recipe box," she said. "I'll bet I could fix us something special for supper."

"I *am* hungry," he confessed.

"Ethan, you were born hungry," she said as she riffled through the box. Her grandmother's familiar handwriting made Leah feel linked to the woman she had loved and lost when she was still a child. Leah pulled up a card. "This one looks easy. If Mom has all the ingredients, we'll be eating in a couple of hours."

Leah studied her grandmother's neat writing and swallowed a lump of emotion. She set to work on the beef stew.

Leah and Ethan ate in front of the fireplace, where Ethan had laid fresh logs. He wolfed down three bowls of stew, and three slices of bread, topping off the meal with two glasses of milk and half a bag of vanilla wafers.

"Get enough?" Leah asked, slightly awed by the sheer quantity of food he had downed.

"Is there more?"

She threw a pillow at him. "Eat this."

Later Leah made popcorn. Close to midnight, she stopped the video they were watching and switched over to network television. Crowds of people were partying in Times Square. Leah found a bottle of sparkling grape juice in the refrigerator. Neil and her mom often liked wine with their dinner, but with Neil's chemo he couldn't drink alcohol, so her mother sometimes served the bubbly grape juice instead. Now Leah filled two of her mother's good wineglasses for her and Ethan.

"Watch, watch!" she said as the great, glowing ball began to descend and the crowd began the countdown.

"They all seem very happy," Ethan observed.

"The start of every year means starting fresh. People like that."

"I am starting fresh, too."

The ball hit the bottom, an orchestra played "Auld Lang Syne," and Leah clicked her glass to Ethan's. "Here's to us."

He sipped the juice while gazing at her over the rim of the glass. "Now what?"

On TV people were hugging and kissing. "We're supposed to kiss for good luck. And wish each other Happy New Year."

He set his glass down and pulled her into his arms. "Happy New Year, Leah."

"Happy New Year to you," she whispered as their lips touched.

"This is a good custom among you English," he said.

His wording jarred her. *You English.* For a while she had forgotten their differences. She warned herself not to forget again. "Well, back to our movie." Her hand was shaking as she clicked the remote. She settled into the heap of pillows and blankets still strewn in front of the fireplace.

"Maybe we should go to our beds. The electricity has warmed the house."

"Maybe later," she said stubbornly, not wanting their time of togetherness to end. "We'll watch some more films—we've got a bunch more." She gestured toward the stack on the floor.

"We would have to stay awake all night."

"So what? We can sleep all day tomorrow."

"Sleep through the day?" He sounded scandalized.

"Okay—half the day. At least until you need another feeding."

He laughed. "It is different not to have

cows to feed, chores that must be done. I'm not used to this."

"We have goldfish," she said. "Want to get up at five in the morning and feed them?"

"No," he said, stretching back against the pillows. "I want to watch movies all night with you. It is a brand-new year, is it not? We can begin it however we please."

Leah had faced the start of other years before, but never had she felt that one could hold so much potential for happiness along with so much room for tragedy. The possibilities whirled in her head. Would her cancer remain in remission? Would Neil win his battle for good health? Would Ethan love her enough to stay in her world? She chased away the list of questions and punched the Play button.

Leah woke with a start. Electronic snow filled the TV screen. It was daylight, but the day looked cloudy, the skies dreary. Beside her Ethan was on his stomach, fast asleep. Groggily she reached for the remote and clicked off the VCR. What time was it anyway?

She heard a noise. With a start, she realized it was a key in the front door. *"Oh, no!"* This wasn't the way she wanted to be found. "Ethan! Wake up!" Leah shook his shoulder.

"Leah! Honey, we're home," she heard her mother call. "Where are you?"

"Hurry!" Leah urged Ethan.

Leah scrambled up. Ethan rose beside her just as Leah's mother and Neil came into the room.

Her mother stopped dead in her tracks. Her mouth dropped open as her eyes swept over the pillows and blankets in front of the fireplace. Her gaze halted on Ethan. For a stunned moment, no one spoke. Finally, in her frostiest tone, her mother said, "Just what is going on here, young lady? I want an explanation, and I want it now."

TWELVE

"I—I can explain," Leah stammered.

"I'll just bet," her mother snapped.

Neil stepped forward. He looked shocked, as if Leah had struck him. His look cut her deeply. She'd rather have done anything than upset Neil. "Is this your friend Ethan?" he asked.

Ethan held out his hand. "I am Ethan."

Neil took Ethan's hand, but before he could say a word, Leah's mother stormed over, picked up a blanket and shoved it at Leah. "Is this what you do behind our backs? Tell us you're visiting a friend, then shack up with your boyfriend?"

Leah felt her face burn with embarrassment. "That's not what happened, Mother—"

"I trusted you!" her mother exclaimed. "Is this how you pay me back?"

"If you'll let me explain—"

"I can't believe it, Leah. How could you do this to us?"

Neil put a hand on his wife's arm. "Calm down, Roberta."

"Calm down? She's not your daughter, Neil. She—" Leah's mother stopped her tirade. "I didn't mean that," she amended quickly. "I'm just so upset."

Neil looked at Ethan. "Why don't I take Ethan and show him my car collection? That'll give you and Leah a chance to clear the air."

Grateful for Neil's offer, Leah nodded vigorously. Neil had a knack for knowing what to say and do in a crisis. And this was a crisis.

"I should stay," Ethan said, looking bewildered. "This is my fault, too."

Leah turned toward him. "Go on with Neil, Ethan. You wouldn't want me around if it were your father's and your discussion. I need to talk to my mother alone."

Ethan hesitated, then said, "All right, I will go. But if you need me, call for me."

She watched Ethan and Neil leave, waited for the click of the front door, then spun on her mother. "That was so embarrassing! You shouldn't have said those things in front of Ethan."

"Well, pardon me," her mother mocked icily. "I always expect to come home from a holiday and find my daughter and her boyfriend sleeping together."

"We were *not* sleeping together!" Leah stamped her foot. "We fell asleep in front of the TV watching movies."

Her mother rolled her eyes. "Oh, please, Leah. Give me some credit. You've been crazy about this boy for over a year. You spent a summer with him." Her eyes grew wide, then narrowed. "Did he spend nights at your apartment? Did we fund your little love affair all summer long?"

On the verge of tears, Leah cried, "How can you think such a thing? I've never slept with Ethan. Sure we've had the opportunity, but we never did. He respects me. He loves me."

"Loves you? What would a seventeen-year-old like you know about love?"

Leah saw red. "I know lots about love, Mother. I know you don't have to marry five times to find it." Color drained from her mother's face, but Leah didn't back down. "I know that love is caring enough about a person to stick around when things get tough. I know that love is letting your daughter see her grandmother. And helping her keep in touch with her real father."

Where did all that come from? Leah wondered. She hadn't meant to say those things. She'd meant only to tell her mother about her and Ethan.

Her mother stiffened, but she kept her voice controlled when she spoke. "I'm not going to discuss ancient history with you, Leah. This is neither the time nor the place. I won't allow you to distract me from the real situation—finding you and Ethan alone and unsupervised in this house."

Leah heard the subtle shift in her mother's words. At least she was no longer flinging wild accusations. Leah swiped at the tears rolling down her cheeks. "I know how it must look, but nothing happened between me and Ethan. You've got to believe me."

"So you say. How can I believe you when the evidence is all over the floor?"

"Don't you think if we were sleeping together, we'd have tried to hide it from you? Not leave ourselves out in the open for you to trip over?"

"I don't know what to think." Her mother rubbed her temples as if fighting off a headache.

"Here's what happened, from start to finish. Just listen." Leah told her mother about the storm, the power outage, their watching TV and falling asleep. When she finished, she said, "That's why we were on the floor. We just conked out."

"That explains the physical situation," her mother said. "But it doesn't tell me why he's here in the first place."

"That's going to take a little longer." Leah sat on the sofa. Her legs ached from holding her body rigid. "He's here because I invited him to stay with us for a while."

"Oh, Leah! How could you? Neil and I don't need some teenage boy underfoot. Especially now."

"Just listen," Leah said. "Please. I told him Neil could help him find his brother." Leah patiently explained about Eli, the estrangement between Eli and Jacob, the terrible sense of loss Ethan felt over the death of his sister and the disappearance of his brother. "I know what it's like to feel alone, Mom. I know what it feels like to want your family intact."

"Is that another slam about the way I raised you?"

"No." Leah sighed. "I'm just telling you what I felt growing up . . . about how much I wanted a family around me."

"*I* was your family," her mother said sharply.

"You worked."

"I had to put food on the table. I had to take care of us."

Leah was tempted to remind her mother again about her tendency to marry any man who came along. She thought better of it. At least her mother had calmed down and seemed to be listening to her. "Look, right now Ethan needs to get some things settled. I offered to help him. I don't see how that's going to interfere with your life."

"Dare I remind you that Neil's recovering from cancer?"

"Well, so am I," Leah said. "And I know that having Ethan around is good for me. Why don't I talk to Neil and tell him just what I've told you and let him decide about letting Ethan stay?" Leah felt confident that Neil would be more sympathetic than her mother.

"I don't want to burden Neil. He—He isn't feeling all that good."

The news jolted Leah. "He's sick?"

A shadow crossed her mother's face but quickly disappeared. "No, I'm sure he's fine. But he's tired all the time. He just hasn't gotten his strength back from all that chemo yet."

Neil's chemo had ended weeks ago. "He was feeling all right at Christmas and before your trip."

"It was probably just the trip," her mother said dismissively. "We were very busy and went to parties with many of his old friends. He's just overextended himself, I'm sure."

Leah stood, suddenly anxious to talk to Neil. "I'm going out to the barn."

"I'm not finished discussing this."

"I want to talk to Neil about it," Leah said stubbornly.

"Oh, all right." Her mother sounded tired and cross. "But this isn't over—not by a long shot. I'm going to unpack. And then there's a meal to think about fixing."

"There's some leftover stew in the fridge. I made it last night from one of Grandma Hall's old recipes. She used to make it for me when I was little, before—" Leah broke off. "Well, anyway, I liked it a lot."

Leah started for the garage, where her coat and boots were.

"Leah," her mother said, "I know you have plenty of questions about the past."

Trust her mother to state the obvious. "You're right. I do."

"Well, be careful. Don't be so eager to dig around in the mud. You might not like what you find."

Without another word, Leah left the house.

In the barn Leah found Ethan and Neil inspecting the cars. Several of the tarpaulins had been pulled back, exposing the fine old machines. Looking keenly interested, Ethan told Leah, "These are very beautiful."

"Not like Amish buggies, huh?"

"Did you pacify your mother?" Neil asked.

"For the moment."

"Ethan explained to me what happened."

Leah studied Neil's face. He looked thinner. "Do you believe us? We weren't doing anything wrong, Neil."

"I believe you both. And don't be hard on your mother, Leah. She's just concerned for you."

Leah said, "Mom and I have some things to work out. But it has nothing to do with you. I'm sorry about her crack about me not being your daughter."

"I know she didn't mean it."

"Which is a big part of her problem. She often says things before she thinks. It hurts people's feelings."

Neil gave Leah a sympathetic smile. "It's a problem for most adults. Especially when they love their kids."

Leah didn't feel like arguing the point. She stared hard at Neil, studying him for a long moment. "Mom said you haven't been feeling great."

"A little tired," Neil said. "Lingering effects of the chemo, I guess."

"It made me tired too, but once it was over, I snapped right back."

"You're younger," Neil said with a grin. "It takes a little longer these days."

"When do you see your doctor again?"

"End of the month."

"Maybe you should—"

"Oh, quit your worrying," Neil patted Leah's hand. "I'm fine. I just need a little rest." He turned toward Ethan, who was listening intently to the conversation. "I know you didn't come all this way for a New Year's Eve party, Ethan. Why did you come home with Leah?"

"I want to find my brother."

Ethan explained his situation; then Leah explained how she was hoping Neil could help him. "There's no big rush," she added. "And we'll do all the work. But we don't even know how to begin."

Neil looked thoughtful. "I'll have to give it some thought myself."

"Not right this minute," Leah said hastily. Neil looked exhausted. "I figured Ethan could stay in the basement, in the extra room down there."

"And I will work, sir," Ethan said. "Anything you need done around your property. I'm a good worker. Plus, I'll get another job to pay for my room and food."

"Oh, I don't think that'll be necessary."

Ethan shook his head. "No. I must work."

Neil nodded. "We can talk about it later. Don't think I didn't notice the clean walk when we drove up. You did a good job."

"Thank you," Ethan said.

"There are lots of little things around the house that need doing. I can do them, but . . . well, my energy level isn't up to par."

"I will do whatever chores you want done."

"Keeping the cars up is important to me."

"All you must do is tell me how."

Neil smoothed his hand over the fender on the nearest car. "I'll be glad to. Forgive an older man's vice, but I love these big hunks of metal."

"I feel the same affection for my father's horse and buggy."

Neil flashed Ethan a big grin. "Then we're not so different after all. You've got a job, Ethan."

Leah watched the two of them shake hands and felt relieved. Ethan was staying.

THIRTEEN

Ethan moved into the basement area of Leah's home, Leah returned to classes and schoolwork, and by the end of the first week, Ethan had proved himself nearly indispensable to the household. While Ethan still didn't have a full-time job, Neil managed to keep him busy caring for his cars and doing minor repairs around the property.

"That young man can fix anything," Neil told Leah.

"And he'll eat anything, too," Leah said. "He eats Mother's cooking as if he actually likes it."

Neil chuckled but admonished, "She's not *that* bad a cook."

Leah didn't argue, but she looked forward to the nights when take-out food was on the menu.

At school Leah settled back into classes, but as soon as the final bell rang, she headed straight for home—and Ethan. He had been with them only a couple of weeks when the two of them drove into town for a movie. They were in the ticket line when Sherry bumped into them.

"Hi," she said, giving Ethan a curious stare.

Leah introduced them. "Want to sit with us?" she asked.

"Love to," Sherry said with a grateful smile.

After the movie they went for hamburgers. The minute Ethan left the table to order more food, Sherry leaned toward Leah. "So this is the Amish boyfriend you used to mention?"

"That's right."

"And you talked your mother into letting him move in with you?"

"It's just for a while. Until he gets some things worked out." Leah didn't tell Sherry about the search for Ethan's missing brother, only that Ethan had some family problems.

Sherry leaned back in the booth and gave Leah an admiring look. "I'm totally impressed. Have you ever thought of politics as a career choice? I mean, if you can persuade your mom to let the guy you're dating live with you, you must be some talker."

Leah laughed. "It wasn't an easy sell, believe me. But Ethan's so nice and he helps around the place so much, even my mother is beginning to depend on him." She frowned. "Still, it would be good if he could get a real job. I know it's starting to bother him that he isn't giving Neil and Mom money for his keep."

Sherry stirred her milkshake with a straw. "Maybe my dad can use him."

"Really? What's your dad do?"

"He's a veterinarian. He has a practice out on Mill Road. He takes care of farm animals—and house pets, too. I help out in the summers, but lately he's been talking about getting someone to help him in the field. Birthing season is just beginning for the farmers. Since Ethan's Amish, he probably knows a lot about animals."

Leah nodded enthusiastically. "He knows tons. Would you ask your dad about giving Ethan a job?"

"Sure. And I'll call you."

"That's really nice of you, Sherry."

Sherry shrugged self-consciously. "It's no big deal. You're my friend. I'd like to help you out. And besides, Ethan's nice. Not to mention totally gorgeous."

"I'll tell him you said so."

Sherry shrieked and her face turned red. "Don't you dare!"

" 'Don't you dare' what?"

Both girls started, then looked up to see Dave Simmons, who had appeared beside their booth.

Leah stiffened, remembering their last encounter. "Private conversation," she told him. "Don't eavesdrop."

Dave held up his hands in mock surrender. "Well, excuse me. The princess has spoken. Let the world stop spinning."

Sherry sat mute as a post, her face reddening even more.

"Leah? Is there a problem?" Ethan had come alongside the table. He set his food tray down.

Dave turned, then gave Ethan a hostile gaze. "Who are you?"

"Ethan Longacre."

Dave looked Ethan up and down. "You aren't from around here. Where do you go to school?"

"I do not go to school."

Leah's heart thundered. She didn't like Dave's attitude. Ethan didn't understand the threat Dave represented.

Dave said to Leah, "I never figured you for falling for a dropout. Or is he just stupid?"

"Get lost," Leah told him.

"I am Amish," Ethan said, as if that would explain everything.

Dave rolled his eyes. "Even worse."

Suddenly Sherry's milk shake slopped across the table, landing on the front of Dave's jeans.

"Whoops!" she cried, looking horrified.

The pale white glop rolled down his pant leg. Dave jumped back, swearing.

Ethan stared at him. "You are rude," he said to Dave. "And we do not want your company."

"Go away," Leah said, "before I call the manager."

People's heads turned in their direction and conversation fell off. Desperately Leah hoped Dave would notice and not cause any more of a scene.

Dave glared menacingly, swore at Ethan and Leah and stalked off. He stopped, grabbed a handful of napkins and mopped his pants. He turned long enough to say, "Listen, Amish boy, if you know what's good for you, you'll stay out of my way."

Ethan turned his back on Dave. "He is not nice."

Leah's hands were shaking. "He's mean, Ethan. Don't mess with him."

Ethan grinned. "He is like a dog locked behind a fence. He barks but has little courage."

Leah started to argue her point, but then

she remembered Sherry. "You all right?" she asked.

"Sure," Sherry said, looking acutely embarrassed.

Leah was fuming. "Dave's a jerk. He shouldn't have said those things. Good thing you had that accident."

"It wasn't exactly an accident," Sherry said with a sheepish grin.

Leah returned her smile gleefully. "Good for you. Too bad you couldn't have dumped it on his head."

"I will buy you another," Ethan said.

"No. . . . It's okay. Really. I've lost my appetite." Sherry stood and slipped on her coat. "I've got to be going anyway. Leah, I'll call you after I talk to my dad. And Ethan, it was nice meeting you. I'm sorry Dave was so rude. We're not all that way."

Leah and Ethan watched her leave. When they were alone, Ethan said, "I am sorry for your friend's feelings. What is Dave's problem?"

"He doesn't like you."

"He does not even know me."

Leah briefly explained how she kept

turning down dates with Dave. "A guy like him thinks he's God's gift to the world. He can't take no for an answer. Still, I'd have thought he would have gotten over it by now."

"His anger is foolish, but it does not bother me."

"It bothers me," Leah said. "You be careful, Ethan. Stay far away from him."

"I do not fear him."

Leah knew it was the truth, but she feared for Ethan. In his heart he was still a plain person, but the world around him was different from his world in Nappanee. In her area, kids might not understand about the Amish. And they might not treat them with kindness. "Just be careful," she said again, feeling the gulf between her and Ethan opening up once more.

On Sunday evening, while Leah and Ethan were playing Monopoly, Neil came and sat down at the table. "Who's winning?"

"Ethan," Leah grumbled. "He has the best luck. Look, he owns all the railroads, plus Boardwalk and Park Place."

Ethan's blue eyes studied the Chance card he'd just drawn. "I have gotten an inheritance of five hundred dollars."

Leah groaned and counted out five Monopoly bills from the bank.

"Let's take a break," Neil said. "I want to talk to you about finding this brother of yours."

Ethan leaned forward. "Yes."

"I've been giving it a lot of thought," Neil said. "Tell me everything you know about him."

"I know nothing."

"Wait," Leah interjected. "Didn't you tell me you ran into one of his old teachers once? You told me she said Eli was finishing college and going to become a teacher."

Neil said, "Did he become a teacher?"

"I do not know."

Neil considered the dilemma. Watching his face, Leah was again struck by how thin he looked. "I'll call the Indiana State Board of Education and ask if there's a teacher in the state named Eli Longacre," Neil said.

"And if there is not?"

"Then I'll contact teaching organizations

in surrounding states. If that turns up nothing, we'll try national groups."

"But what if he is not a teacher?"

"There are other ways of finding people," Neil said. He found a yellow pad of paper in a desk drawer. "Right now, I want you to tell me everything you can remember about your brother." He took notes while Ethan answered his questions. Once he was satisfied, he said, "I won't give up, Ethan. We'll find out something about Eli."

"Thank you for your help. I am in much debt to you."

Neil shook his head. "No debt, Ethan. I know what it's like to want to know about your family. My parents are dead and my only brother died in World War Two. Except for Leah and her mom, I have no family at all. But I've always wanted one. The bigger, the better."

Leah rose and gave Neil a quick hug. His cheek felt dry and papery against hers. "Well, I want to thank you, too. I knew you could help Ethan."

Neil patted her back. "We all need help now and again. I'm glad to be able to offer it to you. You're a good man, Ethan. I hope you find your brother, and I hope you won't be disappointed in what you find."

"How do you mean?" Ethan asked, looking puzzled.

"People change," Neil said. "Sometimes for the worse."

Up until that moment, it had never occurred to Leah that finding Eli might not be a pleasant experience. She locked gazes with Ethan and saw instantly that it had not occurred to him either. Her mother's words from New Year's Day came back to her: ". . . *be careful.* . . . *You might not like what you find.*"

FOURTEEN

At school Sherry told Leah that her dad wanted to interview Ethan for a job, so on Wednesday afternoon, Leah drove Ethan out to Dr. Prater's animal clinic on Mill Road. She parked and was about to get out of the car when Ethan stopped her. "I am not sure this is a good idea, Leah."

"But why? I thought you wanted a job."

"I must have a job. But this is so far from your home. How will I get here if I am even hired?"

Leah sank back into the car seat. "Gosh, I didn't think of that."

"Maybe I should just forget about finding Eli." Ethan sounded discouraged.

"You can't give up already. Neil's hardly gotten started in his search."

"Neil is not well. I can see it whenever I look at him. He does not need my problems."

"But he likes doing this for you, Ethan. And I think he needs to do it. It makes him feel useful. Even my mother is glad for him to have something to do."

Leah was telling the truth. Her mother had done an about-face concerning Ethan's stay at the house. "Having Ethan around makes Neil feel good," Leah's mother had confided to Leah. "It gives him some comfort knowing that little things are being taken care of. Ethan listens to Neil and seems to respect whatever he says."

Leah saw the results of Ethan's handiwork almost every day when she came home from school. In the weeks he'd been living with them, he'd fixed leaky faucets, painted the living room and kitchen, cleared out the garage, and helped Leah's mom sort through boxes full of stuff in the attic and garage. And he took care of Neil's antique cars.

"Don't worry about getting here if you get the job," she told Ethan. "We'll work something out. Even if you have to take me to school every day and use my car."

Ethan nodded, but Leah could tell he wasn't crazy about her offer. It wasn't the Amish way to be indebted to people.

Inside the building, Dr. Prater showed them around. He and Ethan talked about farm animals and what would be expected from Ethan. By the end of the interview, Dr. Prater seemed very satisfied with Ethan's abilities and offered him a job on the spot. "I'll need you five days a week, from eight in the morning until around four o'clock, and half days on Saturdays," Dr. Prater said. "Especially during the upcoming calf-birthing season."

Ethan hesitated, then agreed.

"Good," Dr. Prater said with a smile and a handshake. He went to a file drawer and handed Ethan a sheaf of forms. "Fill out the necessary paperwork, and you can start this Saturday."

At the dinner table that night, Neil and Roberta congratulated Ethan on getting the job, but Ethan shook his head. "I must call Dr. Prater back and tell him I cannot take this job."

Alarmed, Leah set her fork down.

"Why?" Neil asked.

"The papers the doctor gave me asks for numbers I do not have."

"Such as?"

"I do not have a social security number."

"But everybody has one," Leah's mother said. "You can't get a job in this country without one."

"I have only worked on my father's farm. I do not have this number."

Neil leaned back in his chair. "The Amish don't pay social security taxes," he said. "I remember now. They're exempt by congressional order because they don't accept any of the benefits. They take care of their own and have no need of government handouts."

Leah hadn't known this, but it didn't surprise her.

"It is our way to care for one another," Ethan explained.

"Take the job," Neil advised. "We'll apply for a social security card and tell the doc it's coming." He drummed his fingers on the table, a thoughtful look on his face. "This gives me an idea about finding your brother. If he's working, he has to have a social security card, too. That might be a way to track him down."

As long as Neil was in a problem-solving mood, Leah thought she'd bring up Ethan's need for transportation. "He can use my car," she added, "but he'll have to take me to school every day."

"No need for that," Neil said. "He can use my old pickup. You do have a license, don't you?"

"Yes."

"Good. Then it's settled. You can go to work."

"You are too generous. I will not forget all you are doing for me."

Neil dismissed Ethan's thanks with a wave of his hand. "You just pay your insurance and gas. The old truck will need a tune-up before you can drive it, however. I'll take it into a garage tomorrow. There was a time when I could tune that baby up myself, but not now." Neil sounded sad about it. "I could teach you, Ethan, but I guess you don't want to learn how to be a mechanic."

"I would learn—for you. But animals are more to my liking."

Once the truck was mechanically sound, Leah and Ethan went their separate ways each day. Leah missed being with him when she returned home from school, but she made herself do her homework then so that she could have free time with him during the evenings.

Leah arrived home one afternoon to find her mother crying at the kitchen table. "What's wrong?" Leah dumped her books on the floor and hurried to her mother's side.

"Neil's white count is up," her mother said between sniffs. "More than up. It's very high. His doctor wants to put him back on chemo."

Leah felt her stomach sinking. An elevated white blood cell count was ominous in Neil's case.

"It's an experimental drug, part of a test program," Leah's mother said. "They want Neil to try it, although Dr. Nguyen warned us that there may be some adverse side effects."

"What kind of side effects?"

"Nausea, vomiting—there's a whole list. But she wouldn't have recommended him for the program if the other therapy was working."

Leah's stomach churned. She was afraid she might throw up. "When will he start?"

"They'll reinsert the infusion pump tomorrow. He'll have to go for weekly testing, and if he can't tolerate the drug at all, he'll have to go off it." Roberta's gaze flew to Leah's face. "I don't know what I'll do if anything happens to Neil."

Leah was at a loss for words. Her mother was begging her for reassurance, but Leah didn't know how to give it to her. "We'll just have to hope the new drug works," she said lamely. "How's Neil taking the news?"

"He's trying to act cheerful, but he's devastated. I can tell. We both had such hope that the other chemo had worked. Leah, it's been less than three months since he was in remission. I never dreamed he'd have a relapse. And so soon!"

Leah trembled over the note of desperation in her mother's voice. "Where is he?"

"He walked out to the barn. The news has really shaken him up."

A raw February wind whipped Leah's hair as she hurried to the barn. She found Neil inside, seated on the hood of an old Desoto, his head bowed and his elbows propped on his knees. He looked up when Leah came inside. She said, "Mom told me."

Neil managed a crooked grin. "So now I'm a guinea pig." Tears slid down Leah's cheeks. Neil fumbled for a tissue in the pocket of his jacket. "You girls, honestly. You cry like babies, but you never have a tissue handy."

Leah wiped her eyes. "Yeah . . . Imagine crying about you relapsing and going into a high-risk drug program. Go figure." She blew her nose.

He offered a wry smile. "Point taken. Listen, kiddo, these next few months are going to be tough sledding. I don't have any false illusions about this new stuff helping me a whole lot."

"You talk like you don't expect this to work."

Neil sighed. "It's a long shot, honey. A real long shot."

Leah's chin trembled and fresh tears pooled in her eyes. "I don't want you to die."

"I'll stick around as long as the good Lord lets me. I want to live. And I want to stay out of the hospital."

"What can I do to help?"

"You may have to let your mother lean on you a bit."

"Her lean on me?" Leah thought the idea preposterous.

"You know how she sometimes lapses into denial: 'If I don't think about it, then maybe it isn't happening,'" Neil said. "She doesn't mean anything bad by it. It's just the way she copes. You know?"

Leah sniffed. "What do you want me to do?"

"Just be sensitive. Help her adjust." Neil shifted on the hood of the car and lightly slapped the fender beside him. "Hop up."

Leah settled next to him.

"She loves you, Leah. She depends on you."

Leah was skeptical. "Mom's always had someone else in her life to lean on. I sometimes thought she'd be better off if she'd never even had me. I felt in the way."

Neil shook his head. "Not true. Everything she did, every marriage she entered into, was with you in mind."

"Well, except for you, she had bad taste."

Neil chuckled. "Thanks for that." He patted Leah's hand. "Did you know that she never finished high school?"

"She never told me that!"

"She's never told you a lot of things."

Leah was irritated that Neil knew things about her mother that she didn't. "Did she ever tell you why she dumped my father? Or why she hated my grandmother?"

Neil didn't answer right away. When he did, his tone was serious. "Your father suffered from paranoia. Do you know what that is?"

Leah had heard the word used loosely but couldn't remember what it really meant. "I'm not sure."

"It's a kind of mental illness. The victim often suffers from delusions of persecution. He thinks someone's out to get him, that he's the focus of a conspiracy. He hears voices that tell him to do bizarre things. Often the victim seems perfectly normal and completely functional. Then something happens that triggers an episode and he turns into some sort of deranged person."

Leah stared at Neil, stunned by what he was telling her, unable to fully absorb it. *"My* father? You're talking about *my* father? He—He was crazy?"

"He was sick, Leah," Neil corrected.

"Didn't he go to a doctor?"

"Back then there wasn't much that could be done for a person with paranoia. Over time your father got worse, and your mother was afraid. She divorced him because she was afraid he might harm her. Or you."

"And Grandma Hall? What about her? What did Mom say about her?" Leah was shaking. She felt angry and defensive. Parts of her universe were fragmenting in front of her eyes. She'd known that something had been wrong between her parents, but she'd never suspected this. Why hadn't her mother told her?

"Your grandmother had a blind spot when it came to her son. Mothers sometimes do, you know. She refused to accept her son's illness. She blamed your mother. When your father took off, your grandmother tried to get custody of you and failed. It left your mother bitter. She married the first guy who came along out of self-preservation."

Neil took Leah's hand. His hand felt warm; hers was icy cold. "I've begged your mother to tell you all this, but she keeps saying, 'I'll tell Leah someday . . . when she's older.' I think you're old enough, and I'm telling you because she's going to need you to help her through whatever happens to me. I'm also telling you because I didn't confide in you about my previous cancer. I saw how much that upset you."

Leah felt as if she had heard a story about somebody else. It was as if Neil were telling her something he'd read or seen on television. It couldn't really be her life they were discussing. "I—I'm glad you told me," she said, numb from the weight of the information.

Neil said, "I know I've dumped a lot on you, Leah, but you need to start seeing your mother through new eyes, to begin to understand her life and the choices she's made. Most everything she did was for you. Even marrying me."

Leah whipped around to face him.

"Don't be shocked," Neil said. "I've always known, and it's never bothered me."

"But she loves you." Leah's voice sounded small, childlike. "She's told me so."

"I know." Neil smiled. "That's the best part of all. That's how I know she'll be here for me no matter what happens. No matter how bad it gets. We're a family, Leah. For better or worse, we are a family."

FIFTEEN

Neil went into the hospital the next morning and straight into surgery for the reinsertion of the infusion pump. At Neil's insistence, Ethan went on to his job, but Leah skipped school so that she could hang around the waiting room with her mother. Leah had hardly slept the night before. Her mind spun. Not only was Neil facing medical uncertainty, but also, she wondered what the failure of his chemo protocol might mean for her. If she relapsed, would she also have to endure an experimental drug program?

The revelations about her father, mother and grandmother haunted her. How could she have never known the truth? Why hadn't anyone told her until now?

Leah and her mother sat together in an empty waiting room. Her mother sipped coffee and stared out the window at the bleak February landscape. Leah fidgeted, wanting to talk to her mother and not knowing how to begin.

Her mother relieved her of her dilemma when she said, "Neil told me he talked to you yesterday in the barn. He told me everything the two of you talked about."

"You should have been the one to tell me," Leah said, knowing she sounded hurt. "Why am I always the last to know about everything in this family?"

"It isn't a conspiracy, Leah. I was going to tell you about your father. I just never knew how."

"The same way you told Neil. You just say it." Leah paused as another thought occurred to her. "You're not mad at Neil, are you? Because if you are—"

"I'm not mad at Neil," her mother said. "He wouldn't do anything to hurt either of us."

Leah stood, unable to sit still one more

minute. "I know what Neil told me, but I'm mixed up. *You* once told me that the reason you wouldn't let me see Grandma Hall was because you were mad at Dad for not being able to take care of us. You said that you were bitter and that you took it out on her." Leah recalled as if it had been yesterday the conversation she'd had with her mother when she'd been hospitalized. "So which is it?"

"I also told you that your father wasn't well psychologically. That's the closest I ever got to telling you about how sick he really was. I should have told you everything then, but I didn't."

"Why not?"

Her mother shrugged. "If you could have seen the look that crossed your face when I told you as much as I did, you'd know why. You looked horrified. And then hostile, as if you'd never accept anything negative about him from me. You had him built up in your mind to godlike status. You were also being told at the same time by your doctors that you had cancer and that you might lose your leg. I couldn't trash your father to you.

It wouldn't have been right. You needed to concentrate on the future, not the past."

"Why is everybody always trying to protect me instead of being honest with me? Neil said you divorced Dad because you were afraid for our safety. Is that true? Did you think Dad would have hurt us?" It pained Leah deeply to think such things about her father.

"You idolized your father, Leah. You were Daddy's little girl from the time you were born. In spite of everything that happened, I wanted you to have that illusion."

"But it was all a lie!"

"No," her mother said. "When he was in his right mind, it was true. But when he had an episode, when he heard voices telling him to protect you, even if it meant running away with you or hiding you, I panicked. One night I came home from work and he thought I was the Angel of Death come to snatch you away. That's when I moved out. I didn't have any place to go—my parents were dead, and Grandma Hall thought I was a horrible person for deserting her son. I found us a dumpy little trailer in a crummy trailer park, but it was all I could afford. I worked nights, and a neighbor watched you. I married Don when you were five."

Leah remembered the trailer more clearly than she did her first stepfather. He took off when she was six. The trailer remained her home until she was almost seven. When Leah's mother would go to work, Leah would lie alone in the dark, terrified, listening to the sounds of the night outside her window. They had moved from the trailer into an apartment when Leah's mother married her third husband. That marriage, too, had ended in divorce. Leah had been nine. But when Leah was ten, her real father died, homeless and alone in an alley far away in Oregon. Then Grandma Hall died and Leah's mother married for the fourth time.

Leah's fourth stepfather was years younger than her mother, and Leah had disliked him intensely. He left them less than a year later. Then she and her mother lived alone for two years. Finally Neil had entered their lives and had given them both a sense of being cared for. Leah had thought the hard times were finally over. But she was wrong. Now they might lose Neil to cancer.

Leah turned to face her mother. "Neil said Grandma Hall tried to get custody of me. Is that true?"

"She threatened me with a custody battle right after your father and I separated," her mother replied. "Voices had told him that a mysterious stranger was stalking him and was going to kill him. It wasn't true, of course, just another one of his delusions. But he left me with a pile of bills, a child to raise, and no money. I was angry. When your grandmother tried to take you away, I freaked. Of course, we never went to court, but I swore that she'd never see you again."

But she did, Leah thought. Her grandmother had sneaked into Leah's day care centers and schools to visit her. Even now, Leah couldn't bring herself to tell her mother that. "But when she got sick, you took me to the hospital to see her."

"I did," her mother said with a sigh. "I felt sorry for her. She was alone. Her son—

your father—was dead. She had no one else
in the world but you. And I didn't want her
to die without making my peace with her."

Leah realized that many of her notions,
ideas and impressions of her childhood
were not correct. She'd thought her father
had been a sad and lonely man, driven off
by her mother. Her recollections of her
mother's and grandmother's animosity had
been true enough, but now Leah understood their enmity. Maybe her grandmother
had meant well, but wouldn't any mother
fight to keep her only child?

Even her mother's many marriages took
on new meaning for Leah. Her mother had
married to improve her lot in life. Using
marriage to better oneself seemed distaste-
ful to Leah, but she realized that her
mother had probably considered herself re-
sourceful each time. Leah began to understand why her mother had always worked
at menial jobs. Without a high-school diploma, she'd probably had no choice.

From the nurse's desk down the hall,
Leah heard a doctor being paged. Weak
February sunshine pooled on the toe of her
boot. The smell of old coffee hung in the

air. A nurse's aide rattled bedpans as she walked down the hallway.

"So is that it?" Leah asked quietly. "Is that everything there is for me to know about my dad, about the past?"

"Yes," her mother answered. Then she added, "Just one other thing. You may not understand a lot of my choices. You may be angry about the way things went for you as you were growing up. But until you have a child of your own—until you have to make choices and decisions for your child's welfare—please hold back judgment on the way I've handled things."

Leah stared at her mother. At the moment, she couldn't imagine having a child of her own. At the moment, she couldn't imagine even wanting one.

The experimental drug was not kind to Neil. He became deathly sick. His hair fell out. Sores erupted on his body. He lost so much weight that he couldn't wear any of his clothes, and Leah's mother had to buy him a new wardrobe. Once Dr. Nguyen allowed him to go home, Neil stayed in bed, too ill to get up. Leah watched a few of their favorite television shows with him at night, but Neil usually fell asleep. Sometimes he felt so nauseated he had to be helped to the bathroom.

Ethan continued to be invaluable to the household. He did every chore Leah's mother asked him to and continued to keep Neil's cars clean and polished—all while he worked days at Dr. Prater's. His presence brought calm and eased tension in the house. Leah's mother was less likely to fly off the handle when Ethan was around. Leah was more likely to be nice to her mother in Ethan's company. Neil kept saying how grateful he was that Ethan was looking out for them.

Neil apologized to Ethan over his inability to continue the search for Eli. Ethan assured him it was all right. "I'll get back to it when I'm feeling better," Neil promised.

Ethan received letters from his family, and he occasionally wrote letters home. He never shared the contents of his mail with Leah, except to say, "Charity sends a hello to you." It hurt Leah that he didn't, but then she had not told him of her talks with

Neil and her mother, either. She wasn't trying to hide the information about her childhood from him, but she knew it was totally out of his Amish frame of reference. How could he ever relate to a father gone mad? Or to a childhood filled with a regiment of stepfathers? Or to marriage vows broken with the rap of a judge's gavel?

In March Leah received her SAT scores. She was stunned to learn that she had scored high enough to rank nineteenth in her senior class of 321.

"Wow," Sherry said in awe. "I didn't know you were so smart. No offense."

"None taken," Leah said with a laugh. "I didn't know either."

The news gave Neil a spurt of energy he hadn't had in weeks. "Good for you, kiddo," he said from his bed when she told him. A smile lit his haggard face.

Her mother acted especially pleased about her scores. "I always knew you were bright. I read to you every night before bed when I didn't have to go to work."

Leah was ashamed to admit that she didn't remember.

Leah's school counselor called her in to discuss her scores. "Surely you've chosen a college by now," Mrs. Garvey said.

Flustered, Leah answered, "No. I—I'm not even sure I'm going to college."

Mrs. Garvey leafed through Leah's records. "I know that your grades aren't exemplary, but you've brought them up steadily over the past year, and now your SATs prove that you're college material. You really should consider going, Leah. There are many fine colleges and universities in Indiana, if going too far from home is a problem."

Leah had too much on her mind at the moment to do more than nod, thank the counselor and take a sheaf of brochures from her.

In late March, the high school sponsored the Spring Fling, a week of activities that culminated with a carnival on the school grounds. A boy named James asked Sherry to go to the carnival, and Sherry begged Leah to bring Ethan and double-date with them. "I'm scared," Sherry told Leah. "I've never had a date before, and I'd just feel better if you were with me for moral support."

Leah agreed, even though she didn't really want to go. On the night of the carnival, she and Ethan met Sherry and James in the gym parking lot. The four of them headed to the football field, where an enormous tent had been erected. It was packed with kids, teachers and guests. Along the sides of the tent, booths had been set up with games of chance. Proceeds would go toward buying library books and new sports equipment for the high school—"after we split the money with the carnival owners," James said in a tone that assured the others he had privileged information. "And everybody knows these games are rigged in the carnival owners' favor."

"Is that a fact?" Ethan asked innocently.

"Absolutely," James said, pulling his baseball cap tight against his head. "No one can win."

"Then we shall have to un-rig them," Ethan said, heading over to the nearest booth.

"What's he going to do?" Sherry asked.

Leah flashed a smile. "Come see for yourself."

They walked over to a booth where rows of wooden bottles were stacked. "Try your luck," said the man in the booth. "Three balls for a dollar. Knock 'em down and win a prize for the little lady." Leah had gone to a carnival with Ethan in the summer, and she knew how talented and clever he was at the game. The booth tender hadn't a clue.

"Yeah, Ethan," a voice boomed from beside them. "Win the little lady a great big prize."

Startled, Leah jumped. She spun to see Dave Simmons's mocking grin and malevolent glare.

SIXTEEN

Leah stiffened. Dave was the last person she wanted to be near. Cory Nelson, one of the school's more popular cheerleaders, was hanging on his arm.

Ethan offered an open, friendly smile. "Would you like to try first?" he asked Dave.

Sneering, Dave said, "I'm sure I can do better than you, choirboy."

Three of Dave's buddies, who were standing behind him, laughed. Leah wondered if Dave ever did anything without an audience.

Ethan held out the three balls. "You can buy the next set."

Dave took the balls and turned to Cory. "What prize do you want?"

Cory studied the grouping of stuffed animals, then pointed up at a large, bright green dragon. "That would look cute in my room."

Dave nodded, shouldered up to the booth, aimed and threw a ball with such force that it nearly made a hole in the back of the canvas. But his pitch missed the bottles entirely. "Hey, watch it!" the booth tender growled.

Dave glared at him and heaved a second ball at the next stack of wooden bottles. Only the top bottle fell. His friends clapped him on the back and said, "Way to go!"

Dave's third pitch toppled only one more bottle from the third grouping. Dave stared in dismay. "Hey, this thing is rigged!"

Ignoring Dave's outburst, the booth tender asked, "You going to try again? If not, move aside. There's a line behind you."

Ethan stepped up to the booth and looked at Dave expectantly. Dave cursed but pulled out a crumpled dollar bill and slapped it down. "Your turn, choirboy."

Ethan took the balls the man handed

him, eyed the bottles, then lofted a ball toward the first stack. It tumbled backward. He did it two more times, each time toppling a pyramid. Dave and his friends stared open-mouthed at Ethan's effortless accomplishment.

The booth manager said, "You did it, kid. What's your pleasure?"

Ethan looked at Leah. She pointed to the dragon. When the man handed it to her, Leah held it out to Cory. "Ethan wins this stuff for me all the time. Take this from us," she said sweetly.

Dave's expression looked murderous, but Cory, oblivious to the tension among Leah, Dave and Ethan, squealed and grabbed the stuffed animal. "Too cool. Thanks, Leah."

Leah hooked her arm through Ethan's and walked away. Sherry and James, who had watched from one side, joined them. Sherry said, "I think you made Dave mad."

"But why?" Ethan asked. "It was a fair contest."

"Dave doesn't play fair," Leah said. "But so what? He's a creep and I'm glad you beat him."

Ethan stopped. "I did not act kindly toward him. I knew I could win and I forced him to go against me. I did not play fair either."

James snorted. "Quit with the attack of good conscience already. The guy would have humiliated you if he'd won."

"He's right," Leah told Ethan.

"Still," Ethan said, "I should have been a better person. I have been taught, 'Do unto others as you would have them do unto you.'"

"Don't you mean, 'Do unto others *before* they do it to you'?" James laughed at his own joke.

A frown creased Ethan's brow, but he said nothing else.

The four of them continued to stroll around the carnival, but Leah could tell that Ethan wasn't having a very good time. After thirty minutes, she said, "Maybe we should go home. I told Neil I'd be back before he went to bed." It was a half-truth. She knew Neil rested better once she was home for the night, but she also was not much in a party mood. She offered Sherry an encouraging smile and headed outside with Ethan.

By now it was dark, and the March air felt damp and cold. Leah pulled her jacket closer. Ethan slipped his arm around her shoulders. "You are unhappy," he said. It was a statement, not a question.

"I guess the business with Dave upset me. Guys like him should have a belly button check just to make sure they're really members of the human race."

Ethan laughed. "You say funny things, Leah."

"Well, you shouldn't feel bad about winning the game. What's wrong with winning?"

"Nothing. Still, it is a matter of the heart. My heart was not generous toward him. That was not right."

By now they were at Leah's car. She fumbled in her purse for the keys, but before she could find them, bodies materialized from the shadows. In moments she and Ethan were surrounded by the hulking forms of Dave and two of his buddies. Leah gasped and pressed herself against the cold metal of the car. "What do you want?" she cried.

"I just want to talk to your friend here." Dave's voice sounded low and menacing.

"Go away," Leah said, looking around. The parking lot was dark and deserted. With their backs against the car, there was no place to go.

"I'm not talking to you," Dave said sharply. He leaned toward Ethan. "You know what? I don't like you."

"You do not know me," Ethan returned.

Leah didn't think Ethan sounded frightened. Obviously he didn't realize the danger.

"I don't want to know you," Dave said. "I think you're a wimp."

Ethan said nothing.

"Yeah," Dave said, glancing at his two friends. "This guy's a real weenie."

Dave's buddies grunted.

"And you're a jerk!" Leah blurted out. "Leave us alone."

Dave threw up his hands in mock surrender. "The princess speaks." His tone turned nasty as he added, "But I'm not talking to you, Leah. I'm talking to the choirboy." His body tensed and his hands clenched. "Why don't we see what you're made of, choirboy?"

Still Ethan said nothing.

Alarmed, Leah stepped between them. "Please, go away. Ethan's done nothing to you."

Dave shoved Leah out of the way. One of his friends caught her and held her arms behind her back.

"Let her go," Ethan ordered.

"Why? You going to do something about it?"

Leah struggled, but she was held fast. Her fear gave way to anger. "Let go of me!" she bellowed. "He's just trying to provoke you, Ethan. Don't let him."

Dave shoved hard on Ethan's shoulder. "Your girlfriend always tell you what to do?" he asked. "You let a girl run your life?"

Ethan didn't move, even with Dave's shove. It must have maddened Dave because he shoved him harder. Ethan stood like a rock, his hands hanging loosely at his sides. With an open hand, Dave slapped Ethan hard across the face. Leah cried out, but Ethan still didn't budge.

"What's the matter?" Dave snarled. "Can't you make a fist?"

"I will not fight you."

Lightning fast, Dave smacked Ethan's face harder. The sound of the slap crackled in the cold night air.

"Stop it!" Leah cried. Why didn't Ethan defend himself?

Dave jabbed at Ethan's face. Ethan bobbed his head to miss the blow. Dave jabbed again. This time, the blow connected. Ethan's head snapped back hard, but he still did nothing to defend himself. "What's the matter?" Dave asked. "You too chicken to fight?"

"I do not fight," Ethan said.

"Then I'll beat the crap out of you where you stand," Dave said, moving forward, fists jabbing at Ethan's head. Braced against the car, Ethan couldn't get out of Dave's way. "You're a coward," Dave said, dancing and jabbing. "Come on and fight!"

Leah brought the heel of her boot down hard on the toe of the boy who held her. He yelped and loosened his grip, and Leah started swinging. She clobbered Dave hard on the side of the head.

"Why, you—" He started toward her.

"What's going on here?" A voice boomed from the darkness.

All movement stopped, and the football coach hurried up to the group. "I asked what's going on. Simmons? What are you doing?"

Dave leaped back, brushing his knuckles on his jeans. "Nothing."

Leah was shaking so hard that she could barely make her voice work. Her hand throbbed from striking Dave. "He attacked us," she said.

The coach stepped forward and peered at Ethan. "Is that true? Are you all right?"

"I am all right," Ethan said quietly.

The coach spun toward Dave. "I don't know what happened here, but I do know that fighting on school grounds is forbidden. You're up for several athletic scholarships, Simmons. Don't make me put this on your record. You save the hostility for the football field, you hear me?"

"Yes, sir."

The coach looked at the other two boys. "I expect to see all three of you in my office first thing Monday morning. Then I'll decide what your punishments will be. Now, the three of you get out of here." Dave and his friends backed away. "This is finished," the coach added. "Do I make myself clear?"

Shaking with anger and frustration, Leah watched Dave and his friends go. "I hate them," she said.

"I'm sorry," the coach said. "But don't worry; I'll deal with them. You two sure you're not hurt?"

"We're okay, I guess." Leah sniffed hard. When the coach left, she turned to Ethan.

"Let's go," he said.

Inside the car, with the dome light on, she saw that his lip was bleeding and his eye was beginning to swell. "You're hurt."

Ethan blotted his lip on his sleeve. "It is nothing."

"Why didn't you stop him?"

"Amish do not fight."

"I know that, but you could have at least defended yourself."

"I will not fight, Leah."

"Not even to defend yourself? Or someone you love?"

He shook his head. "Leah, my feelings about violence cannot vanish simply because I am threatened. What good is a virtue if it is untested? What good is a belief if any challenge causes us to toss the belief aside?"

"But you could have been really hurt!"

"Often God provides a way out. Tonight the coach showed up."

"But what if he hadn't shown up?"

"But he did," Ethan said.

"Well, you almost got your teeth knocked out." Leah started the car and gunned the engine. "And I can't believe you Amish don't make allowances for hitting a bully like Dave who's about to do you bodily harm. You'd think you could at least defend yourselves!"

"It is our way, Leah." Ethan's tone sounded patient, as if he were explaining something to a child. "It has always been our way. It always will be."

She gritted her teeth, afraid to answer him because she was so angry. How could anybody stand by and let some idiot pound him into the ground and not lift a finger? Some things about the Amish made no sense to her at all. "I'll put some medicine on your lip when we get home," she said. "Or is that against your rules too?"

He said nothing. They didn't speak for the rest of the ride home.

SEVENTEEN

Scuttlebutt at school the next week had it that Dave and his two friends were in deep trouble. They could have been suspended, but the coach intervened and they were spared. For punishment, they had to pick up trash and paper from the school grounds every day after school for two months. They steered clear of Leah, which suited her fine. But she couldn't forget the fear she had felt and Ethan's absolute refusal to do anything to protect them.

"Would it have been better if he had fought and gotten pounded to a pulp?" Neil had asked her when she told him her feelings.

Leah shuddered at the image of her tender, gentle Ethan after a bashing by Dave. "Of course not. But what about the next time some jerk comes along and threatens him? Will he never stand up for himself? I see bad stuff every day on TV. Sometimes a person has to fight. Or die."

Neil sighed. "I agree—the world's a mean place. But the Amish are pacifists and always have been. They don't fight in wars. If they must serve in the military, it's in a noncombat support role."

Ethan had once told Leah the same thing, but at the time she'd hardly paid attention. Now she couldn't shake her fear that something awful might happen to Ethan if he never did anything to protect himself.

Neil added, "This is one of the reasons that the Amish keep to themselves—so that they won't have to fight and quarrel. Their world and ours don't mix. You've known that all along."

Yes, Leah had known it, but now the disparities between her and Ethan's worlds had taken on a sinister note. This time it was more complicated than not using electricity or modern conveniences. As for Ethan, he went about his everyday life as if nothing had happened. Neither Leah nor Ethan spoke of it again.

Leah was out in the barn helping Ethan with the cars late one afternoon when Neil came in to see the two of them. His gait was little more than a shuffle and he was slightly stooped, but Leah could tell he was excited about something. "What's going on?" she asked.

Neil waved a piece of paper. "Ethan, I think we've found your brother."

Ethan dropped the rag he was using to polish chrome and hurried up to Neil. "Eli? You've found Eli? Where is he? Can I go to see him?"

"Whoa . . . One thing at a time." Neil thrust the paper into Ethan's hand. "This is a report concerning him. It appears he changed his name to Elias Long. That's why it took so much time to track him down. I hadn't thought about his renaming himself, but he did."

"This will shame Pa," Ethan said, shaking his head.

"I'm sure Eli had his reasons. Anyway,

here's the good news. He's a schoolteacher, and he's employed in the southern part of the state, in a small rural school district not far from the Kentucky border. His address and phone number are in the letter."

Ethan stared at the paper, but Leah saw a slight tremble in his hand. It was Ethan's only outward sign of excitement. "Do you want to call him?" she asked.

"No. I want to see him. With my own eyes, I want to look into his face. Will you come with me, Leah?"

Leah and Ethan left on Saturday. Since the trip was about two hundred miles, Ethan asked off from work and Dr. Prater excused him. Ethan said little during the drive down the interstate. He drove while Leah watched the countryside fly past as they headed south. Pale pink blossoms adorned plum trees, and new leaves sprouted from trees like insets of green lace. Tulips and daffodils pushed through the hard, dark earth in spikes of brilliant color. Even the cold air was tinged with the scent of spring.

"Are you excited?" she asked.

"I have dreamed of this for years, but now that it is about to happen, I feel . . . well, like there are butterflies inside my stomach."

"He's probably missed you as much as you've missed him."

"I am not so sure. If he wanted to see me again, he would have come home."

Leah had no reassuring words to offer.

Once they were off the interstate, Leah checked the map and the directions a gas station attendant had given them. "I think that's it up on the right," she told Ethan. A lone mailbox stood by a gravel driveway that led to a house set far back on the property. "Yes, this is the place," she said, checking the number on the mailbox.

Ethan turned onto the driveway.

"It sort of looks like your place," Leah said. "Not the house, but the property." A garden could be seen off to one side, and clusters of trees dotted the land.

"I am surprised," Ethan said. "Eli always hated working in the garden." He stopped the car behind a pickup truck parked in front of a garage. His knuckles looked white on the steering wheel.

A dog bounded from around the side of the house and started barking. Fearlessly Ethan got out of the car. Leah waited patiently while Ethan made friends with the big black Lab. When she thought it was safe, she got out and, with Ethan, walked up to the house. The dog trotted at their heels.

The front door opened and a man stepped out onto the porch. He was tall and thin and dark-haired. His eyes were blue, like Ethan's. His features were hauntingly familiar to Leah, although she'd never seen him before in her life. Leah knew he was around twenty-five, but he looked much older. He asked, "What do you want? Are you lost?"

"Eli?" Ethan said.

The man stared. Color drained from his face. "E-Ethan?" he stammered. "Is it you, Ethan?"

"Hello, my brother."

"Dear Lord. It *is* you." Eli staggered backward. "I never thought . . . I mean . . . How are you? What are you doing here? How did you find me?" His flood of questions stopped abruptly. "Is it Pa or Ma? Have they—?"

"They are well," Ethan interrupted. "I have come on my own. I have come to see you."

Suddenly Eli swept Ethan into his arms, buried his face in Ethan's neck, and began to cry.

Fifteen minutes later Leah and Ethan were inside the house sitting on a worn sofa. Ethan had explained about Leah, about Neil's search, and about his coming into the English world with Leah's help. "It took a very long time to find you because you changed your name," Ethan said.

"I wanted to be more like the English," Eli said, his eyes still shining with emotion. "It was easier to fit in if I used a more English-sounding name. And at the time, I didn't want anything to do with the Long-acre name."

Leah saw that the confession hurt Ethan. "And are you like the English?" he asked.

It was a needless question. A television set in a bookcase, piles of books and videos, wall-to-wall carpeting, lamps and a computer on a desk painted a clear picture. There were also toys, blocks and a game board scattered in one corner of the room.

"Nice place," Leah said, smoothing over the awkward moment. She pointed to the toys. "Do you have kids?"

"Sure do. My wife, Camille, and the two boys, Jason and Timmy, are grocery shopping. They should be back any minute now. Hey, would either of you like something to drink? Soda? Coffee?"

They both accepted a cola.

"You look great, Ethan," Eli said, handing him a can. "You've grown up."

"You have changed also," Ethan said.

"Yeah, I guess so."

"How long have you been married?"

"Five years now. Camille works at a day care center. Jason's almost four and Timmy's just turned two. I'm a teacher. But you know that." Eli grinned self-consciously. "I teach high-school English, and I'm planning on graduate school as soon as the boys get a little older. I want a Ph.D. in

education. I'd like to teach college someday."

"You have many plans," Ethan said.

Eli cleared his throat. "What about you?
School?"

"I am finished with school. I was not a
student like you. Or Charity."

"Charity!" Eli exclaimed. "How are our
sisters?"

"They are well. Charity is very pretty—
almost grown. And Elizabeth is already
thirteen. Sarah is married and has a new
son. Simeon is growing tall."

"Simeon was Timmy's age when I left."
Eli got a faraway look in his eye. "Is he still
as blond as you?"

"Yes," Ethan said. "And there is also Na-
than."

"Ma had another baby?"

Ethan nodded. "Ma also had Rebekah.
She died last summer, when she was six."

"Died!" Eli looked stricken. "But how?"

Briefly Ethan told Eli about Rebekah's
short, sweet life. "We miss her very much,"
he added.

"That's how Ethan and I met," Leah

said. "Rebekah and I were in the hospital together, and we got to be friends. I'm sorry you never knew her. She was the sweetest, nicest little girl in the world."

Eli raked a hand through his hair. "I'm sorry too," he mumbled. "And—um—the others?"

"Oma is ill. The winter has been hard on her," Ethan said.

"Pa never got electricity in that old barn of a house, I guess." Eli's expression hardened.

Ignoring Eli's question, Ethan continued, "Opa still works with Pa. The crops have been plentiful these past two years. Yet the old ones are predicting a hot summer— maybe a drought."

Just then the door banged open and a small boy hurtled into the room. "Daddy!" he yelled. He stopped abruptly when he saw Leah and Ethan.

A younger boy trotted through the open door, followed by a long-haired woman carrying a sack of groceries. "Whose car?" she asked.

"Camille," Eli said, "I want you to meet my brother, Ethan."

Camille allowed the grocery sack to slide to the floor, her expression wary. "Hello," she said. "Eli's told me about you."

Leah watched Camille as Eli explained what was going on. It was obvious that Camille wasn't thrilled to see Ethan. She was a small woman with plain features, and she wore a tiny cap on her head. Leah had spent enough time in Nappanee to recognize that Camille was Mennonite, a member of a more liberal religious group than the Amish. While the Mennonites held to many of the traditional Amish values, they believed in using modern conveniences and didn't mind mingling with the English.

The toddler, Timmy, started rummaging through the forgotten sack of groceries. Jason hung on to his father's pant leg, peeking around it with serious blue eyes. Leah saw the family resemblance in Eli's sons. Both boys looked like their father, who looked a lot like Mr. Longacre.

Eli took both boys by their hands. "I want you to meet your uncle Ethan."

Ethan crouched so that he was face to face with the children. "Hello, Jason. Hello, Timmy."

Jason continued to act shy, but Timmy grinned and gave Ethan a hug. The gesture tugged at Leah's heart. With his winsome, open smile, Timmy reminded her of Rebekah.

"You must stay for supper," Camille said in a tone that told Leah she'd rather they wouldn't.

"Yes," Ethan said. "This would be good. I have much to learn about these years we have been apart."

"You could stay the night," Eli said. "We'll put the boys in with us. Leah can have their room. Ethan can take the couch."

"All right," Ethan said without hesitation.

"I'll call Mom and Neil and let them know," Leah said.

"Well, let's help unload the groceries," Eli said cheerfully.

A look passed between Eli and Camille that Leah caught. She'd seen her mother pass enough such looks as she was growing up and read it instantly. It said: *Why are you doing this? I don't want them here.* Leah felt instant rejection but also firm determination. Ethan had come too far and worked too hard to lose his brother now. He deserved to get to know Eli—whether Eli's wife liked it or not.

EIGHTEEN

Later Leah found herself sitting on the sofa with Ethan, listening to Eli tell of the years between his leaving home and the present.

"College was difficult," Eli said as he flipped Timmy's sponge basketball from hand to hand. "Not because of the studying, but because I didn't fit in anywhere."

"I do not understand," Ethan said.

Leah understood perfectly, but she listened to Eli's explanation without commenting.

"When you're raised Amish, you just don't slide into the English world so easily."

"But so many of your friends were English back home."

"True, but they were also small-town and raised around an Amish community. I wasn't quite prepared for dorm life, for all-night parties where everybody got blasted, or for drugs."

"You took drugs?" Ethan looked appalled.

"I tried them, but they weren't for me." Eli gave a sardonic chuckle. "You know what they say, 'You can take the boy out of Amish country, but you can't take the Amish out of the boy'—or something to that effect."

"Why did you hate our way of life so much? How could you leave us and never write? Never come home?"

Eli flipped the basketball across the room and sank into his chair, his fingers laced in his lap. "You know as well as I that when you leave, you aren't welcomed back."

"You could have come home. Pa and Ma would have forgiven you."

"I couldn't go back, Ethan. I hated the farm. I hated living in the eighteenth century instead of the twentieth. I was never accepted by the other Amish boys. Books were my only true friends. When I opened a book I could escape into other worlds by myself. I sailed with Ulysses. I climbed Mount Everest. I traveled to other planets—all within the pages of books. I didn't like slopping out pigpens, pitching hay, plowing fields. I hated the long, boring church services. And most of all, I hated the hypocrisy in our community."

Ethan's face colored. "I, too, have disliked some of the rules, but it is not so bad."

"It was bad for me. Do you remember Jonathan Meyers?"

Ethan shook his head.

"He was the blacksmith until he was shunned."

"Shunning is only done to bring a person back into fellowship."

Eli rolled his eyes. "That's the party line. Do you know what his crime was? His hat brim was one inch wider than the bishop allowed. And for that 'crime' he was ostracized. He was driven away by his neighbors, forced to sell his farm and move."

Leah was shocked. The size of a man's

hat brim hardly seemed like a reason to destroy his life. This was the part of Amishness she could never accept—the complete smothering of individuality.

"He had only to repent—"

Eli thrust out his hand. "Don't start, Ethan. How could this be a crime? How can we, whom the church teaches not to judge, judge so harshly?"

"It was his pride that set him apart. It is pride that can get a man shunned."

Eli scoffed. "Well, I liked Brother Meyer. I liked his daughter, Ruth, also. I was in seventh grade and madly in love with her." A smile of remembrance touched his face. "When she moved away, I thought the world would end."

"I do not remember this," Ethan admitted. "But we have a new bishop now. He is not so traditional as the old one."

How so?, Leah wondered, but she kept quiet.

"Ethan," Eli said with a sigh, "it does not matter. I didn't want to live among such people. I threw myself into schoolwork. I was happy inside my books. I was smart, and in the English world I was admired just because I was smart. At home I was considered prideful and rebellious. You know how Pa can be."

"He allowed you to go to high school."

"So what? We argued about it all the time. But by that time I knew I didn't want to remain Amish. I was ashamed of my backward family and their simple ways." Eli shifted forward, leaning toward Ethan and Leah. "Look at you, Ethan. You are dressed English. You are with an English girl. I know you've had the same feelings."

Leah stiffened. She had often felt guilty about Ethan's decision to take his fling. If it hadn't been for her, perhaps . . . "I wanted to help Ethan," she said defensively. "He wanted to take his fling."

"Trying out English things and leaving Amish ways forever are not the same thing," Ethan said. "And as for Leah"—he turned toward her on the sofa—"she means much to me. She has made my life happy and good."

"But I'm not Amish," Leah added. "You don't have to keep reminding me." Turning to Eli, she said, "I've had to deal with your leaving too, Eli. Your father's very distrustful of everybody English. The only reason your family allowed me to come around last summer was because of Rebekah."

"She must have held extraordinary power over him to have persuaded him to let you within a hundred yards of his precious farm," Eli said.

"Pa is changed," Ethan insisted. "He has suffered much over your leaving—and Rebekah's dying."

"I'm sorry about my little sister. I can't change that. But as Jacob Longacre's eldest son, I don't believe Pa will ever forgive me. I do not want to be a farmer, Ethan. I can't be what he wants me to be. I never could."

"Yet you have chosen what most Amish men choose. You have a wife and a family," Ethan pointed out.

"Do you really think Old Order Amish would accept my Mennonite wife?" Eli shook his head. "I don't think so."

"You will not know unless you take your family back home."

Eli stood abruptly. "No way." He left the room.

Later, while the boys watched a video and
Camille prepared dinner, Leah and Ethan
took a walk. "I guess you didn't persuade
Eli to go home for a visit," Leah said.

"I did not." Ethan looked dejected.

"But still, you've gotten to see him again.
Isn't that what you wanted?"

"Yes. But I also wanted him to return
home. It would mean so much to Ma. And
to Oma, too. She is sick and old. I know it
would make her happy to see Eli before she
goes home to the Lord."

In truth, Leah felt pretty down herself.
She didn't know what Ethan was thinking
or what was going to happen now that he
had accomplished his goal of reuniting with
Eli. "Have you ever felt like Eli did? I
know your father didn't want you to take a
fling. I know he wasn't thrilled about your
seeing me."

"I have had many arguments with Pa,
but taking a fling is my right. Seeing you is
my pleasure."

"And you don't see how this is a double
standard? That you're going against Amish
convention?"

Ethan turned, took Leah by the shoulders and pulled her close to him. "I do not know how it will all turn out, Leah. I only know I love you."

She threw her arms around him and buried her face in the hollow of his neck, where his pulse throbbed and sent her pulse soaring. "What's going to happen to us, Ethan? What are we going to do?"

He did not answer.

After supper, while Eli bathed the boys, Leah helped Camille wash the dishes. The kitchen was small and painted bright yellow. Jason's and Timmy's drawings hung on the refrigerator, attached with colorful letter magnets. Someone had spelled out *cow, cat, dog.* "Jason?" Leah asked.

"Timmy, actually," Camille said. "He's only two, but can already pick certain words off the pages of books. He's going to be smart like his father."

"Where did you meet Eli?" Leah asked.

"College. We both have education degrees. I'll go to work once the boys are in school so that Eli can return for graduate work."

"Sounds like you have everything planned out."

"I like having a plan." Camille put a pot into the suds. "How about you? What are your plans?"

"I don't have any." Leah told Camille about Neil. "I think I should hang around until I see how it's going to work out."

"Are you thinking that you might have a life with Ethan?"

Camille's question was unexpected and made Leah stammer. "I—I don't know."

"Well, take it from me, Leah, living with an Amish man is not easy."

"You do it."

"And it has been difficult. Eli has such guilt about not seeing his family. Despite his feelings about his Amish upbringing, he is not free of it. He tries to be English, but he can't quite let go of his Amishness. He is caught between the two societies, and I tell you, on some days it has threatened his sanity."

"This afternoon he talked as if he hated everything Amish."

Camille wiped her brow, leaving a trail of suds near her hairline. "What he hates is not being able to get rid of it. If it were a tumor, he could go to a surgeon and have it cut away. But it's imbedded in him, even now, after all these years of being away. It would be the same for Ethan. No matter how much he loves you, he will always be bound to his culture."

Leah felt her cheeks growing warm. Until now, no one had ever paired her and Ethan in a permanent way. Even she had hesitated to project a future for them. "Do you hate the Amish?" Leah asked.

"I grew up in Ohio, near an Amish settlement. I am Mennonite—a people sometimes not regarded highly by Amish because we rejected many of the old ways decades ago. I have seen firsthand how conflicted the Amish children are when they attend English schools. Our sons and I have suffered with Eli as he has tried to find his way between the Amish and English worlds." Camille paused, staring gloomily out the window over the sink into the blackness of night. "Still, I do believe it's not good for Eli to totally reject his family. I have suggested many times that he make peace with his father and go back for a visit.

Perhaps seeing Ethan again will help him decide to do it."

"I know it would mean a lot to Ethan."

"Well, if you love Ethan, Leah, be careful. Don't think you can make him forget his past. Don't think your love can make up for all that he holds dear in his heart. If you do, you will only find your own heart broken."

Leah slowly dried the glass bowl she held, not daring to respond to Camille's comments. Ever since she'd first met Ethan, she'd been attracted to him—and to the sense of family he brought with him. The Longacres were close-knit and involved with one another, not estranged and cut off as she'd often felt in her own family. That is, at least until Neil had become a part of her and her mother's lives and offered a stability Leah hadn't known before.

Over the summer, Leah had lived among the Amish, but she knew she'd not been fully accepted by them. A part of her found their lifestyle attractive, even compelling. Another found the Amish full of contradictions. They were a people of great personal integrity and strong family values.

But poor Ethan! She didn't want him to end up like Eli: torn and divided, unable to make his peace with either the world of the Amish or that of the English. Neither did she want to feel forever like an outsider herself, as Camille did. Leah found it difficult to think about a future with Ethan, and even more difficult to see her future without him.

NINETEEN

That night Leah slept fitfully. She was glad when the aroma of brewing coffee drifted up from the kitchen. She got up, dressed and went downstairs, where she found Eli and Ethan sitting at the kitchen table.

"Good morning," Ethan said with a smile. "I have told my brother that we will leave this morning. I must work tomorrow, and you have school."

"Do you like school?" Eli asked Leah politely.

"It's all right."

"Leah scored high on those SATs,"

Ethan offered. "She is near the top of her class."

"Good for you," Eli declared. "Where are you going to college?"

"No plans yet. I've never loved school the way you do."

"Don't waste your talent," Eli said. "I see many students who are smart but unmotivated. They're headed for dead-end lives. College helps you focus on your future."

Leah wasn't in the mood to discuss her future. "I'm thinking about it," she said, pouring herself a cup of coffee. It gave her something to do with her hands. "I'm sure Ethan's told you about my stepfather, who is so ill. I'm not sure I should make too many plans." She didn't mention her own medical baggage. "Anyway, I haven't decided what I'm going to do yet." She sat down at the table. "You know, Eli, you have nice kids. And back in Nappanee, you have some really nice brothers and sisters. That means that Jason and Timmy have some pretty neat aunts and uncles. Because I grew up alone, I think it's cool to have a big family. I think you and Ethan are both lucky to have that. For what it's worth."

Eli wrapped his hands around his coffee mug. "I'll take your comments under advisement."

Leah smiled sweetly. "Just as I'll take yours about college for me."

Timmy and Jason swooped into the room, clamoring for breakfast, and soon Camille joined them. She prepared a big batch of pancakes, which the group wolfed down, and once the dishes were cleared, Leah and Ethan prepared to depart for home. Soon Ethan and Leah were standing in the driveway and Eli and his family were clustered around them.

Ethan opened the driver's side door and got in.

"So you have your license," Eli said. "Does Pa know?"

"No," Ethan admitted.

Eli shook his head. "He's still as hard as ever."

"No, he is not," Ethan insisted. "Go home and see for yourself. You will be surprised."

Eli leaned into the window. "I can't do

that, brother. I can't let him subject my family to his unbending, unyielding attitudes. It would confuse my sons and undo everything I've spent these years trying to forget."

Leah leaned over to look Eli in the eye. She said, "He didn't put up a fight when Ethan made up his mind to come home with me in January. It upset him, sure. But he let Ethan go without any yelling or arguing. I think you should know that."

"That's hard to believe."

"It is the truth," Ethan said.

Leah added, "I always wished I'd had a grandfather, but both of mine were dead by the time I was old enough to know what one was."

Eli straightened. "I'm glad you came, Ethan. You are a fine man. I have missed you."

"And I you."

"Will you write?"

"I will."

"You are welcome to come again," Camille offered, hooking her arm through Eli's. "Both of you."

Eli nodded. "Yes. Now that we've rediscovered one another, please don't lose touch." Leah saw moisture in Eli's eyes and felt sorry for him.

"You are my brother, Eli. Nothing will ever change that. Not ever."

As the car pulled out of the driveway and onto the highway, Leah watched through her window until Eli and his family vanished from sight.

When they reached home, it was night and rain was falling. The house's windows were dark. "Wonder why Mom hasn't turned on any lights," Leah said. "She knew we were coming home."

Ethan raised the garage door. Roberta's car was gone. They went into the house, but the silence told Leah that no one was home. In the kitchen, she found a scribbled note taped to the refrigerator door: *Neil took very sick. Ambulance came. I went to hospital to be with him. Come ASAP.*

Leah's heart sank, and nausea gripped her stomach. "Something's wrong with Neil, Ethan. We have to get to the hospital. Hurry!"

Together they ran out the door into the rain.

Leah found her mother in the emergency room waiting area. "Mom! What happened?"

Roberta grabbed Leah's arms. Her face looked pinched and white. "I went to take Neil his supper tray. I couldn't wake him up. I was scared. I called nine-one-one and an ambulance brought him here. He's unconscious, Leah. They won't tell me anything."

"They will when they know something," Leah said. "You'll see. Is Dr. Nguyen with him?"

Roberta nodded and looked at Ethan. "I'm glad you're here too."

"I will stay for as long as you need me."

Leah began to tremble. She couldn't get warm despite the jacket she wore. She kept remembering last summer and the frantic hours of waiting for word on Rebekah.

"I thought he was doing better," Leah's mother said, half under her breath. "I really did."

They waited almost an hour longer before Dr. Nguyen came through the swinging doors of the emergency room's triage
area. Roberta sprang to her feet. "What's
going on?" she cried. "How's my husband?"

"We've finally gotten him stabilized," the
doctor said. "I've transferred him up to a
room."

"I have to see him."

Leah's mother almost bolted, but the
doctor stopped her, saying, "Neil's condition is extremely critical, Mrs. Dutton. His
liver function tests are poor. His liver is fail-
ing."

Leah said, "But without his liver working—" She stopped as the implications
slammed into her.

Leah's mother shook her head. "I won't
accept this. What about that fancy new
drug he was taking? He was doing better
on it. He was."

"The drug didn't have the efficacy we
hoped it would."

Leah wondered why doctors always re-
sorted to using complicated words when

they wanted to sidestep an issue. "You mean it didn't work," she said.

With a slight nod, Dr. Nguyen acknowledged and accepted Leah's remark.

Roberta snapped, "We'll talk more later. Right now, I want to see Neil. Where is he?"

Dr. Nguyen gave them Neil's room number, and with a swish of her coat, Roberta stalked to the elevator.

Neil lay on a hospital bed hooked to IVs and lead wires attached to monitors. His skin, stretched over his thin frame, was the color of mustard. Even the whites of his eyes were yellow. Yet he managed a wan smile when Leah, her mother and Ethan came into his room.

"I'm not too pretty, am I?" he asked.

Roberta bent and kissed his cheek. "You look good to us. Goodness, you gave me a fright. When I came in and couldn't wake you . . ." She didn't finish the sentence.

Neil held out his hand to Leah. "I'm glad you're back and can be with your mother." To Ethan he said, "How'd it go with your brother?"

"It was a good visit. Thank you for all your help."

Neil nodded, shut his eyes and grimaced with pain. "Sorry," he said moments later. "They've given me enough morphine to stop an elephant, but it still hurts."

Leah thought she might burst into tears. "Mom only got to talk to Dr. Nguyen for a few minutes. She said the drug you've been taking hasn't worked."

"I know. It doesn't look good for me, honey."

"Stop that kind of talk!" Roberta said with a stamp of her foot. "Your doctor will think of something. I'll make sure she does."

Leah saw resignation on Neil's face. He turned his head toward Ethan. "I need you to watch out for things at the house while I'm laid up."

"I will be there."

"If you need anything—if anybody needs anything—you call Harold Prentice, my attorney. You understand?"

"We will," Leah said.

"Now, you all go on home tonight. I don't want you hanging around this place."

"Fat chance!" Roberta dragged a chair over to Neil's bedside. "I'm spending the night right here with you."

"You need your rest, Robbie."

Ignoring Neil's words, Leah's mother said, "Leah, I do want you and Ethan to go back to the house. Both of you stick to your regular schedules. School tomorrow for you, young lady."

Infuriated, Leah shook her head. "I want to stay, too."

Her mother stood, took Leah by her elbow and dragged her into the hall. "I won't have Neil thinking we're on some kind of death watch."

"But what if—"

"I'll call you if there's any change. You can be here in a matter of minutes. Now please, do as I ask."

Leah felt torn. She knew her mother was right. Neil needed the kind of moral support that came with people going about their normal routines. "All right," she said reluctantly. "But call me if anything happens."

Leah and Ethan said goodbye and left the hospital, but once back home, Leah got scared. "What if he dies?" she asked Ethan. "What if I can't talk to him again?"

Ethan put his arms around her and rested his chin on her bent head. "Do not think such terrible thoughts, Leah. Neil's in God's hands, and God will decide what's best for him. I have an idea," he added softly. "Why don't we bundle tonight? Just as we did on New Year's Eve."

"Here, in front of the fireplace?"

Ethan lifted her chin with his forefinger. "I would like to hold you tonight, Leah. I would like to be close to you and feel you close to me."

Without hesitation, she nodded. Some Amish customs made perfect sense, and on this night she wanted to be in Ethan's arms more than anything. "Hold me, Ethan," she whispered. "I'm so cold. Please, hold me."

TWENTY

As the days dragged by, the three of them fell into a routine. Leah's mother spent nights at the hospital on a cot in Neil's room, remaining through the day until Leah got out of school. Then Leah relieved her mother, who went home to rest, freshen up and deal with phone calls and mail. In the evenings Ethan drove Roberta back in her car and visited until ten o'clock; then he and Leah drove together to the house in Leah's car.

Leah could hardly concentrate on her classes, but fortunately her teachers cut her a lot of slack. Sherry sent her cheerful notes at school and mailed a card to the house.

Leah began to appreciate what a good friend Sherry was and swore she'd be more available to do things with Sherry once Neil had returned home.

However, Dr. Nguyen gave them little hope that Neil would ever go home. "His liver function keeps falling," the doctor said outside Neil's room on Thursday.

"Do something!" Roberta demanded.

"We've done all we can," the doctor said, looking upset. "The cancer's invaded other parts of his body. It's everywhere now, and we can't stop its progression."

Roberta stifled a cry. Tears swam in Leah's eyes. Ethan gripped Leah's hand so hard that it throbbed. "I just can't believe there's nothing else you can do," Roberta said.

"I wish there were. Doctors like to heal patients, Mrs. Dutton, not watch them die."

Leah's mother looked resigned. "What's going to happen now?"

"He'll gradually slip into a coma," Dr. Nguyen said, "which may last a day or a week. But eventually he'll simply stop breathing. I'm sorry. So very, very sorry. He put up a good fight."

"A fight that he can't win is no fight at all," Leah's mother said bitterly.

One afternoon Leah was alone in the room with Neil when she heard him say her name. She dropped the magazine she was reading and leaned over his bed. "Yes? Are you in pain? Do you want me to call a nurse?"

"No. I want to talk to you."

"I'm listening."

"It won't be long now, Leah."

"Please, Neil, no—"

"Now, don't you fall apart on me. I'm not afraid to die, Leah. I know where I'm going from here. But I sure hate leaving you and your mother alone." He sighed deeply. "I need you to watch out for your mother once I'm gone."

Leah wanted to say, "Mom's able to take care of herself," but didn't.

"I know you think she's strong, but she needs you. I love her," Neil said softly. "And don't you ever doubt for a minute that she loves you. She may not have always expressed it in ways you understood, but she's tried to do what was best for the two of you."

Leah had to admit that she and her mother had gotten along much better since Leah had learned the truth about her real father and grandmother. Hearing about her mother's early struggles had helped Leah to understand her mother's proclivity for marrying and divorcing. "You helped make her different," Leah said. Neil had made *both* their lives different.

"No," Neil said. "I only helped make her feel safe." He closed his eyes and Leah thought that he might have fallen asleep, but soon his voice came again. "And watch out about Ethan, too."

"But why?"

"He's Amish, honey. It's in his blood." Neil reached for her hand. "I don't want your heart broken."

"Ethan wouldn't do that to me."

"Not intentionally. But sometimes circumstances come up against us like a brick wall. Circumstances we can't do anything about."

"I know," Leah said. "Like getting cancer." She recognized those kinds of circumstances all too well. But loving Ethan was her choice. "Are you saying falling in love is like getting sick?"

Neil smiled. "Sometimes it seems that way . . . but no. Falling in love is a good thing."

"I know that Ethan and I have a lot of things going against us. I didn't set out to care about some Amish guy, you know."

"I believe you. Too bad we don't always get to pick who we love. Sometimes love just happens to us, whether we're looking for it or not. But finding the right person at the wrong time can be a problem. Lots of things have to come together before love, and the person we love, are just right for us."

Leah wanted to keep talking about herself and Ethan, but she knew Neil didn't have the strength for it. "Maybe you should rest."

"Not yet." His breathing sounded labored. "One more thing." He gestured toward the drawer of his bedside table. "Open it."

Leah discovered a small wrapped box. "What's this?"

"Part of your graduation gift. I had your mother bring it here so that I could give it to you."

"But I don't graduate for two months."

"I won't be there, Leah."

"Maybe you will," she countered stubbornly. "You could fool your doctors and go into remission again."

He slipped his hand over hers. "That's not going to happen, honey. I won't be around for a lot of things in your life. I'll miss your wedding day when that rolls around. But I promise I'll be looking in on you when you walk down that aisle."

Until then, Leah had never considered that she'd have no father to give her away. Tears of sadness and regret filled her eyes. "Then I'll walk alone."

"Sh-h-h. Don't cry now. Just open that box while I can still see your face."

With trembling fingers, Leah opened the box. Inside was a gold charm of a diploma, sparkling with a ruby chip. "For your bracelet," Neil said.

"Thank you. I-It's beautiful."

"No—thank you," he said with difficulty. "I'm so proud of you, Leah. You're smart. You have a good, kind heart. Do something wonderful with your life."

Neil drifted off to sleep, and Leah bowed her head and cried.

Leah and Ethan went to the hospital coffee shop that evening, ordered hot chocolate and sat at a corner table. Leah felt weary to her bones. Neil had not awakened again all afternoon or evening.

"I'm sorry," Ethan said. "I know this waiting cannot be easy for you."

"It isn't easy for you, either," Leah said. "I keep thinking back to Rebekah's death. It happened so suddenly. And with Neil, we've known for months that he was sick, but I'm not any more ready for him to die than I was for Rebekah."

Ethan reached across the table and laced his fingers through hers. "We cannot change what God has ordained, Leah. We may not understand why, but even if we knew why, knowing would not stop it."

"It just isn't fair. And it makes me mad," she said.

Ethan smoothed her cheek with his palm. "But miracles happen also. You are proof of that."

Ever since Neil's hospitalization, Leah had suppressed fears about her own health. She would go for another checkup at the end of May. "But what if—?"

Ethan silenced her with a shake of his head. "You will be fine. I believe this with all my heart."

Not wanting to speculate about it, she asked, "Tell me something to make me happy. I'm so tired of talking about cancer and dying."

Ethan looked thoughtful. "Dr. Prater has offered to send me to a special school this summer in Indianapolis so that I can learn more about veterinary medicine."

Leah sat up straight. "Really? Why didn't you tell me sooner?"

"He only just mentioned it yesterday."

"Indy's not that far away. Hey, you could even commute from our place." She felt a mounting excitement.

Ethan grinned. "You are like a horse with a bit in its teeth—off and running. I am not sure I will go."

"Why not? It sounds like a good idea. You like working with animals. Maybe you could be a vet like Dr. Prater."

"It is much like college for you—a choice, but not one I'm sure I want to make."

"You should seriously think about it," Leah said, her heart hammering. Ever since their visit to Eli's, she had been afraid Ethan would leave. Now it appeared that he had a perfect reason to remain. Besides, the Amish needed veterinarians, so it wasn't as if he could never return to his community. Why, she believed that even Jacob Longacre might approve of Ethan's becoming a doctor for animals. If Ethan stayed the summer and attended the school, then continued working with Dr. Prater, she could stay around too. They would be together.

Leah cleared her throat. "Well, I think it's a great opportunity, and you should really think hard about it."

Ethan stared pensively out the window. "I will, Leah."

On Friday Neil slipped into a coma. Leah got the call at school. She ran out of the building, hopped into her car and sped to the hospital. Ethan arrived less than an hour later, still muddy from a field. "I was helping Dr. Prater with the birth of twin calves," he explained.

Roberta took Neil's hand into hers and kissed his palm. "We're here, honey," she told him. "We'll be here until you leave."

Leah experienced déjà vu. Hadn't she just stood by Rebekah's deathbed only months before? Hadn't she felt these same emotions, numbness, anger, fear, and unbearable sadness? How much grief could a person take?

She asked Ethan, "What should I pray for?"

"Pray that his passing is gentle. And quick."

She bowed her head but couldn't form the words—not even mentally. She didn't want Neil to die. She didn't want to let him go.

The three of them stationed themselves around Neil's bed. They talked to him, touched him, watched his body shut down. Machines performed the tasks of his diseased organs. Time became fluid as the hours melted into one another. Still there was no change in Neil's condition. Nurses brought two sleeping chairs into the room for Leah and Ethan, and then very early in the morning, Leah was startled awake by the high whine of Neil's heart monitor. She leaped to her feet to join her mother, already bent over Neil's motionless body.

A nurse rushed in and flipped off the monitor. The silence seemed deafening. The nurse felt for a pulse. "He's gone," she said.

Leah crumpled onto the bed, sobbing, her lips pressed against Neil's ear. "I love you, Neil." Suddenly the words were not enough. And they were the wrong words. "Daddy," she choked. "I love you, Daddy. I love you."

TWENTY-ONE

Dawn had broken when Leah and Ethan walked out into the cold spring air. Leah's mother had remained to fill out paperwork and told them to wait for her in the lobby. But Leah couldn't stand being in the hospital one more minute. Outside she shivered, and her cheeks, still wet with her tears, felt stiff and frozen. Ethan put his arm around her and they stood huddled together.

Leah said, "I half expected Gabriella to show up and save Neil. Wasn't that stupid of me?"

"How do you know she didn't?"

"I sure didn't see her. Did you?" Leah didn't hide her sarcasm.

"Just because she did not show herself to you does not mean she did not come. I believe she came to take Neil's soul to heaven."

"Why do you think that?"

Ethan pulled back and gave Leah an inquiring look. "Do you not know what today is, Leah?"

"I—I don't even know what day of the week it is."

"It is Sunday. Easter Sunday."

Astounded, Leah asked, "It is?"

"Yes. It is a day for resurrection. It is a good day for angels to come and take Neil home."

Later Leah and Ethan went to the funeral home for the viewing. Leah sneaked off to an unused room and sat, feeling numb and overwhelmed.

Ethan came into the semidarkness and sat down beside her. "I missed you."

"I couldn't stand it in there one more minute. I had to get out."

"So many tears," he said. "So much sadness."

Leah turned to him. "You're thinking about Rebekah, aren't you?"

"Her memory is all around me," Ethan confessed. "Amish, English—the pain is just the same."

"You liked Neil, didn't you?"

"*Ya,* he was a good man, Leah. Yet today, it is not just Rebekah and Neil I am thinking of. I am also thinking of Eli. He is alive, but he acts as if he is dead to us."

"That's the way it was for my real father for so many years. He was alive, but he might as well have been dead for all the good it did us. I wanted him to come home so much." The memory brought on fresh tears.

"Home," Ethan said, with a longing in his voice that made Leah's breath catch.

She reached out and held tightly to his arm. "Stay with me, Ethan. Please, don't leave me now."

He touched her cheek tenderly. "I will not leave you, Leah. I will not."

———

After the funeral the next day, Leah's mother cried softly into a handkerchief. "I miss Neil so much. I feel so alone without him. Like part of me is missing." She sounded desolate.

"We'll be with you," Leah offered.

"Yes," her mother said, as if seeing her for the first time. "Yes, you will. It's just us again, Leah. Only you and me."

Leah wasn't sure how to respond. Neil's death had left a hole that neither of them knew how to fill. They got into the car and rode home in silence.

Guests arrived bearing casseroles and baskets of food and flowers. Leah and Ethan escaped to the solitude of the barn, and being around Neil's cars brought Leah a measure of comfort. Ethan began to methodically polish the steel and chrome of the old automobiles.

"Neil won't be back to inspect them," Leah said forlornly.

Ethan glanced at her with sad blue eyes. "This is true. But I know he would want them cared for if he were here. I will keep them up for him."

How like Ethan, Leah thought. He did

his duty with such a sense of purpose. She felt purposeless, adrift, like a sailor marooned on a far-off island. What was going to happen to her and her mother now?

She watched Ethan polish the cars until it was dark and all the people had left the house.

Two days after the funeral, Roberta came into Leah's bedroom, where Leah was lying on her bed. Her mother asked, "Can I sit for a minute?"

Leah moved over to make room.

"I've just returned from Mr. Prentice's office—you know, Neil's lawyer." Leah said nothing, and her mother continued. "We went over Neil's will. He left everything to me."

"Congratulations," Leah said without emotion. "What will you do with it? Move?"

Her mother looked surprised. "This is home, Leah. I'm staying right here."

"Oh." Leah wasn't sure what she'd expected her mother to say, but she was pleased her mother was staying put, relieved that this would still be home.

"Neil left you something too, Leah."

Leah propped herself up on her elbows. "He did?"

Her mother held out a small gift wrapped in colorful tissue. "Neil wanted me to give you this after . . . well, after he was gone. It's a graduation present."

"He gave me the gold charm at the hospital."

"This is something else he wanted you to have."

Leah unwrapped the present and found a small key. "What's this?"

"It's a key to a safe-deposit box. In it are the titles to all the cars in his antique auto collection."

"What am I supposed to do with his cars?"

"He left instructions that the proceeds from selling the cars should be used to set up a trust fund for you. Those cars are worth a great deal of money, and all of it will be yours to use however you want."

Stupefied, Leah stared at the small key. "Neil did that for me?"

"Yes. He loved you like a daughter. Naturally, it will take some time to find buyers for all the cars, but eventually you'll have quite a nest egg." She paused. "You know, Leah, it was always Neil's hope that you would go to college. Now you have the means to do so."

Leah's mind was in turmoil. "I—I can't think that far ahead now."

Her mother patted her hand. "I understand. But please think about it. You know, I never had a decent education, and my life's been . . . well, difficult. Not that an education will make things perfect for you, but it might make things easier." Her mother stood. "Think about it. We can discuss it if you want." Her fingers trailed across Leah's hair and down her cheek. "I miss Neil very much. He was the best thing that ever happened to me. I'm sorry we had so little time together but grateful that we had any at all."

Once her mother had left the room, Leah's mind raced. She had a trust fund. She had money. Suddenly nagging thoughts about her health nibbled into her consciousness and began to erode her awe and pleasure. She wanted to talk to Ethan. She wanted him to help her decide what to do.

Leah hopped off the bed, went down to the basement and knocked on his bedroom door. "Can we talk?" she asked. "I have some big news."

"In a minute," he called.

"I'll wait for you on the front porch."

Outside, the afternoon sun was lowering over the fields. The spring air smelled fresh and clean. She sat in the wooden swing, fidgeting, eager for Ethan to come. She heard the door open and turned just as he stepped out onto the porch. The smile faded from her mouth. Her heart lodged in her throat.

He was dressed Amish.

TWENTY-TWO

"**W**hat are you doing?" Leah could hardly get the words out.

"I must go home."

"But this is home!"

"This is *your* home," he said, shaking his head. For the first time she noticed how long his hair had grown. And he now wore it as he had when she'd first met him. "I miss my family, Leah. I have to go back to them."

His words hit her like blows. She wasn't enough for him. Why couldn't she be enough? "But I need you, Ethan. How can you leave me so soon after Neil's death?" It was as if her whole world were disintegrating.

He crouched in front of her and tried to take her hand, but she pulled back. "It has been Neil who has helped me understand where I belong."

Leah listened, unable to accept what Ethan was saying. Neil knew how she felt about Ethan. He wouldn't have urged him to leave. He wouldn't.

"All this time of being around Neil, working for him, talking and listening to him, seeing how hard he fought to live, made me see that a person's life cannot be lived independently of those he loves. Neil wanted you and your mother close to him. He wanted to give you all that he could of himself and of whatever time he had left. Neil was like a father to me in many ways. He reminded me of all the good things that my father stands for." Ethan reached up and raised Leah's chin so that she was forced to look into his eyes. "I am Amish. Just as my father is Amish, and his father before him, and all the fathers before that."

"Eli seems to have adapted." Leah's voice quivered. "He made the decision to break from the Amish."

"Then perhaps I can be the one to bring him back."

"That's dumb! He'll never go back."

Ethan stepped down off the porch and scooped up a handful of soil. He returned and held it out to her. His hands were big, callused, and stained by the heavy, dark soil. "This is my life, Leah. Already Pa has begun to plow the fields. He will plant soon. And Ma will start her garden." His voice was filled with yearning. "I love the land. It is in my soul."

"You belong here, Ethan. With me."

"I cannot stay." He let the soil drop through his fingers. It pattered onto the wooden floor.

"But what about your job with Dr. Prater? And that school he wants to send you to?"

"I will write and tell him I cannot accept."

"It's a way for you to be something else. Somebody else." Tears were pooling in her eyes. She had thought she'd cried them all out over Neil, but this fresh supply came from another area of her heart.

"I must return to my world."

She sprang to her feet. "I've seen your world, Ethan. It's a small, narrow world with no room for change. No room for people to think for themselves or to be different. It's a boring world!" She bounded down the steps and ran out into the field. She ran until she thought her lungs would burst. When she stopped running, she sank to her knees and buried her face in her hands.

Ethan was beside her in seconds. "Leah—"

"Don't touch me!" She twisted away.

"Please."

"I thought you loved me."

He grabbed her shoulders and squeezed until she winced. "I do love you. I've never loved anyone as much as you. Leaving you is like leaving half of myself behind—the half that laughs and loves and will always remember the world of the English. You are right—my world is small and narrow. And to some, it is even bleak and backward. But it is my world, Leah." His eyes burned holes into hers. "Your world is big, and you have so much of it yet to see."

"I want to see it with you." She started to cry.

He cried too. "Oma is very sick, Leah. My family needs me. And I need my family. I do not want to be as Eli. He belongs nowhere."

Belonging. It all came down to belonging. She, of all people, understood what Ethan meant. She hung her head and struggled to regain her composure. "When will you go?"

"There is a bus I can catch to Indy. Another will take me to Nappanee."

"No." Leah shook her head dully. "I'll drive you home. I brought you here. I'll take you back."

Leah's mother expressed surprise and regret at Ethan's announcement. Leah had hoped she would say something to persuade him to stay, but she didn't. She merely hugged him and told him he'd always have a place to come to if he ever changed his mind.

Unable to sleep, Leah roused Ethan after midnight and said, "Let's get it over with."

He asked her to let him drive because it would probably be the last time he ever did so. The trip was long, but for Leah not nearly long enough. She did not tell him of the trust fund, mostly because the money would not impress him. He would be happy for her, but it would mean nothing to him.

It was close to five A.M. and morning was already turning the slate sky pink when Ethan stopped at the edge of the Longacre property. He got out of the car slowly. Leah watched him look across the partially plowed fields at the old farmhouse that had been home to his family for more than a hundred years. Flickering lights could be seen through the kitchen window. The household was rising. High up on the second floor, in the window of Ethan's room, a lone lamp glowed. His mother had kept her promise.

A lump of emotion clogged Leah's throat. "You're home," she said.

"Would you like to come in?"

She shook her head. "Not this time."

"What will you do?"

"Drive back."

"The trip is long. You should rest first." He looked concerned.

"I can make it." She started to get back inside the car, but he caught her arm and crushed her against his chest. "Oh, my Leah. I miss you already."

"You'll get over it." She squeezed her eyes shut. Her heart hurt.

He held her at arm's length. "I will never forget you. And I will never love another as I have loved you."

"Your fling is over. You'll be baptized. You'll marry an Amish girl," she said with resignation.

"You were not part of my fling," he said fiercely. "You were part of my life. You will always be in my heart, Leah. Until angels close my eyes."

His face blurred through her tears. "Go," she said. "Go back. Go home."

She watched him as he hopped over the split-rail fence fronting the road. She watched him walk quickly toward the house, toward his family, and out of her life forever.

TWENTY-THREE

The road stretched long in front of Leah. She followed it in a trance, driving by rote, every cell in her body feeling numb. Her world lay in shambles. Neil, the only father she had ever loved, was dead. Ethan was gone, lost to her forever, claimed by his Amish heritage. She had no one. Nothing.

She began to rouse herself from her stupor when her eyelids threatened to close. Realizing that she needed to take a break, she picked up some fast food at a drive-through restaurant window, then got back on the highway and drove to a rest area.

The rest area looked clean, but it was

crowded with people. Some had settled on blankets and were having picnics. Kids ran and played. A family tossed a Frisbee to one another. The spring day, scented with new growth and sun-kissed air, only depressed Leah more. How could the world be so happy when she felt so sad?

Leah found a deserted picnic table near the edge of some woods and sat down heavily. She opened the bag, but the smell of the food made her feel queasy. Still, she tried to eat it. She had another three hours to drive.

"Whatcha doing?"

The little girl's voice startled Leah. She turned to see a child of about five looking at her from a nearby pathway.

"Eating lunch," Leah said.

"I ate lunch already."

"That's good." Leah wished the girl would go away. She just wanted to be by herself.

"My mom and me are running away," the little girl said.

Startled by the child's admission, Leah asked, "What are you running away from?"

"Everything. That's our car."

Leah glanced around and saw a battered old car with a trailer hooked to its rear bumper. The back door of the car stood open, and a woman was rummaging inside for something. "Oh, you mean you're moving," Leah said.

"My dolls and my bed and my toys are locked up. We're taking them a long way off. But I'm not scared." She offered Leah a brave smile. "Mom says I'm her big girl. Mom's got a job in . . ." She looked thoughtful. "In someplace. I can't remember."

Leah suppressed a smile. "Where's your dad?"

The child shrugged. "He went away." She looked sad momentarily, then cocked her head. "Do you like french fries? I do."

Leah was about to offer her one when the girl's mother came hurrying over. "Cindy! Cindy, I told you to stay near the car." She stooped by the child and took her by the shoulders. "Stop going off and scaring me. And stop bothering people."

Cindy's lip stuck out and Leah quickly said, "It's all right. She's no bother."

The woman stood. "You can't turn your

back for a minute." She looked both apologetic and embarrassed. "I've told her a hundred times not to wander off."

"I was just about to offer her some of my fries. Is it all right?"

The woman looked tired and worn out. "That would be nice of you."

"Here, Cindy." Leah held out the small bag. "Take a bunch."

Eagerly Cindy helped herself. She and her mother thanked Leah; then they hurried to the car. Leah watched them with memories of her own many moves flipping through her thoughts. At the car, Cindy said something to her mother; the mother nodded, and Cindy raced back to Leah. "This is for you," she said. She held out a perfect white feather. "I found it."

Leah took it. "Why, thank you. It's very pretty. It must have come off a beautiful bird."

"It didn't come off a bird. It fell off an angel's wing," Cindy explained patiently. "My mom told me so. It's from our guardian angel. She's with us on the trip, you know."

A lump formed in Leah's throat. "Are you sure you want to give it to me?"

Cindy grinned. "I have two." She darted back to the car and climbed in, and Leah watched until the car and trailer pulled out of sight. Thoughtfully Leah returned to her car. She placed the feather on the seat beside her and stared at it for a long time. Finally she started her car and left the rest area.

As she drove, Leah couldn't get Cindy out of her mind. *So trusting,* Leah thought, *confident that her angel and her mother will always take care of her. Just like my mother has always taken care of me.* The thought took her breath away. True, they had never had a family like Ethan's. But they'd had a family. They *were* a family. Through all the turmoil, moves, marriages, and changes, Leah and her mother had always been together. And her mother had fought off every adversary that had threatened to keep them apart.

Leah considered her life. Like the feather beside her, it could blow away in an instant. What couldn't change was who and what she was, who and what she had become through the adversity of cancer, her father's desertion, Neil's death, Ethan's love. No one could see into the future, but all at once Leah knew she had a future. A gift given to her by Gabriella, Neil, Ethan, her mother and even her grandmother. She could have it, if only she would reach out and take it. Yes, she hurt. Yes, her heart felt battered and bruised. But bruises healed. Hearts mended.

Determination began to replace her depression. And when she turned into the familiar driveway, she wanted to see only one person. She wanted to be held just like a small child. She wanted to cry. Then, in a few days, she wanted to sit down and make some plans. Her mother would help her, Leah was sure.

Leah picked up the feather, jumped out of the car, and hurried to the front door. Throwing it open, she called, "Mom! I'm home."

And in the deepest part of her heart, Leah Lewis-Hall knew it was true.

Believe in the power of love

How Do I Love Thee?
THREE STORIES

ISBN: 0-553-57154-0

How do I love thee? Let me count the ways. . . .
These well-known words ring true
for three young couples in this moving
collection of stories.

On sale October 2001 wherever books are sold.

www.lurlenemcdaniel.com
www.randomhouse.com/teens

BFYR 285

DON'T MISS A HEAVENLY TRIO FROM

Lurlene McDaniel

0-553-56724-1

0-553-57112-5

0-553-57115-X

Follow the inspirational story of 16-year-old Leah, as she faces serious illness and falls in love with a young man whose simple Amish values collide with her "English" world. Is there someone watching over Leah? Can she face the tragedies and triumphs that lie ahead?

ON SALE NOW WHEREVER BOOKS ARE SOL

BFYR

n unforgettable new novel from

Lurlene McDaniel

0-553-57091-9

*n one afternoon Beth's entire world is torn away from her
when an accident claims the lives of everyone in her
mily. Beth wishes she were dead too but must find out how
to go on with her life now that she's a "survivor."*

n sale April 1999 wherever books are sold.

www.randomhouse.com

BFYR 211

Get *online* with your *favorite author*

www.lurlenemcdaniel.com

The official
*Lurlene
McDaniel*
Website!

- *interactive author forum*
- *exclusive chapter excerpts*
- *contests and giveaways*

and much more!

BFV